LOUD

A Strong Story

By Damon L Smith

@Freshoutent

This is dedicated to

You with

Three Kisses

Chapter One

It seems like yesterday that my Uncle Percy told me that "the definition of love is that which you go through with somebody". But that was before he died, before I got shot, before I went to prison for 14 years and before the series of very unfortunate events that led me to where I was in life.

"What's wrong Day?" Latoya questioned as she laid across my bed naked as the day she came into this world.

"Shit." I answered over my shoulder as I continued to look out my bedroom window at nothing in particular. "Do I look like something is wrong with me?"

"You look like a 6'1 tall, dark, and handsome Roman statue, with the prettiest smile I've ever seen." She paused to look me over. "But it's not what you look like; it's the way that you are acting."

Latoya had been blessed and cursed with the pleasure and displeasure of being a part of my life for the last couple of months. The fact that she was almost my height, thick in all of the right places, with a beautiful caramel complexion to match her hazel eyes didn't really impress me. But when I found out that she like women just as much if not more that I did, I gave her just enough of myself for her to become addicted to me, and she has been a part of my relationship rotation ever since.

"How am I acting babe?" I asked as I retreated from the window and lay across the bed next to her.

"You act like you ain't happy Day." She responded while at the same time moving herself closer to me. "It's your birthday and you acting like you did when Ace died. So tell me what's wrong babe, and I promise I'll do whatever you want me to do to make it better." She finished as her lips met mine.

"I doubt that very seriously." I thought, but I kept my comment to myself as I enjoyed her kisses.

The thought even crossed my mind to explain to her that almost twenty years ago to the day my favorite Uncle Percy 'Pimpin' Stokes was laid in his final resting place. I also wanted to tell her that all of my happiness and birthday joy went into the ground with him, but I couldn't bring myself to do it. There were only a few skeletons in my closet that she knew about, and I was truly in no rush to make her fully aware of the cemetery that came with dealing with me.

Pulling her closer to me until our skin was touching in more places than not, I decided to leave the words alone and focus on actions instead.

Letting my hands explore the softness of her body, I returned her kisses. One after another after another after another, until her mouth opened to invite my tongue to enter.

Accepting her invitation without the slightest hesitation our tongues danced with each other while my hands touched, rubbed, and grabbed at any part of her that I could reach. She was extremely responsive to my touch, and moaned with every movement as my hands toured every spot on her body that stimulated her in some type of way. Some responsible for more pleasure than others, but each caress brought her closer to her breaking point.

In no rush to satisfy the need that my lips and hands had caused her, I continued to tease her with kisses and touches while I slowly repositioned myself into one of complete control and dominance.

"Don't move." I whispered in her ear as I pinned her to the mattress.

When her breathing had returned to almost normal, I released my grip on her wrist and began to place sweet kisses from one side of her neck to the other. This caused her to start moving all over again, so I pinned her back to the bed as I began to let my kisses work their way down her body.

By the time I made it to her breasts, she was panting and trying very unsuccessfully to maintain her composure. Each kiss seemed to send an electrical shock through her body causing her to jump or shake as I made my way towards her center.

Unable to hold her down and continue with the mission that my mouth had started, when I made it to the top of her landing strip I changed my gentle approach to a more aggressive maneuver, and in one fluid motion went from holding her arms against the bed to holding her thick thighs open.

This put me face to face with her lower mouth, and before her body had the chance to respond to my first movement we were engaged in a one sided tongue kiss of sorts.

Aroused in a way that words could not explain, as my tongue danced across, between, and inside of her lower lips, she spoke to me in a form of broken English that was barely understandable. I wondered to myself what exactly it was that she was trying to say to me, but I was more focused on what I was doing along with keeping her from shaking free from my grasp to be truly concerned. This seemed to happen every time I put my mouth on her in the right way, so I used it as motivation as I dove all the way in search of her climax.

Knowing exactly what would push her over the edge and give her the release that was building up inside of her with each kiss, suck, and flick of my tongue, I gave her lips one last peck before moving on to her love button.

After taking it into my mouth I sucked it slow and soft at first. That lasted for a few moments, but as it got better and better for the both of us, I sped up my rhythm and added more pressure. I went faster and faster, harder and harder until she couldn't hold back or control herself any longer.

Twisting turning, pulling, shaking, rolling, screaming, and hollering, she went through all of her usual responses before her climax caused her orgasmic fluids to leak from her body uncontrollably. Each drop tasting better than the one before it, I held her in the position she was in until I had devoured all of her climatic nectar. And try as she might to break from my clutches, she made no progress in getting away from my oral lip lock until I was certain that she had nothing else to offer me in that department.

My cell phone must have sensed that she really needed a break from what was happening to her, because as soon as I released her from the position that she was in, it began to sing to me "Hey now".

I got 50 for you Day." The caller informed me.

"Where you at?" I questioned.

"I'm on the highway coming through downtown." The caller answered.

Taking a second to look at the phone to ensure that I was talking to exactly who I thought I was talking to I instructed the caller "Get off at Goodfellow, buck a right, then call me" before ending the call and sitting my phone back on the nightstand.

I hadn't planned on going anywhere once I got started on Latoya, but money always moved me. It made my life work right, and that was a priority that I held in high regard. Regardless of who I was with or what I was doing.

"Who was that Day?" Latoya questioned with a hint of hostility in her voice.

"You already know who it was when the phone rang." I paused just long enough to get out of the bed with her. "So please don't act like you don't know what I do for a living."

"Are you serious nigga?" She screamed. "I can't believe you would leave me like this over a few punk ass dollars!"

"It's not the first time babe, and I'm certain that it won't be the last." I explained as I walked out of the bedroom into the bathroom.

"I can't stand yo black ass!" She yelled at me along with several other things, but as the bathroom door closed, so did the sound of her voice.

After adjusting the water to just the right temperature, and the shower heads to just the right function, my thoughts drifted to other things as I bathed myself.

I had only been out of prison for almost a year before I fell right back into my routine like I never left, because hustling was all I knew. It was all I ever knew. I had accepted that fact without even giving it a second thought after I couldn't get a job worth having my first month back in society.

The state provided three hot meals and a place to sleep while I was their ward, but when they finally decided to release me, it was all on me. Nobody cared if I starved other than me, and I refused to miss even one meal regardless of the situation. Because unlike most people the time I spent stuck in a cell in some part of the State of Missouri (pronounced 'Misery') wasn't wasted doing nothing or anywhere close to it.

I actually learned a new way to learn. And when I did, I read anything and everything that I could get my hands on because I figured out a way to get something meaningful out of it that I could use to my advantage later in life. Those lessons helped me to clearly understand several things about people and places that every hustler should know and use to his or her advantage on a daily basis.

Life from that point on was just one simple experiment after another on the predictability of people. But with each new endeavor that I found myself trying to pull off or perfect, I also figured out that my basic formula for each case only needed to be tweaked just a little bit in one way or another depending on which group of people my endeavor actually catered to.

It took me years to admit to anyone other than myself that I was a drug dealer with no personal preference for the poisonous product that I pushed to the people in pursuit of paper. And a decade and a half in the Department of Corrections hadn't changed a thing.

"Babe yo other phone ringing." Latoya called into the bathroom breaking me from my train of thought.

"Who is it?" I responded a little louder than I think I needed to as I turned the water off and exited the shower.

By the time I made it to the phone I had missed the call, so I took a few minutes to dry off. When I finished with that I picked my phone up and scrolled through my call log and found that I had a plethora of missed calls, notifications, and text messages.

Every text had something to do with the fact that it was my birthday in one way or another. Some wished me happy b-day. Others questioned my plans for the day. And the rest were multimedia messages filled with pictures of birthday cards, people singing happy birthday wishes, and a host of other birthday material.

Strangely none of them moved me in any type of way, so I made a mental note to respond to them all at a later time, then I tossed the phone back on the nightstand next to the other one.

"Day can you explain to me again why you have more than one cell phone?" Latoya questioned as I was getting dressed.

I had told her on more than one occasion that I never mixed business with pleasure and that I kept a separate phone for each product I sold. It made hustling a little bit easier for me, because I basically knew about what the caller on the other end wanted when the phone rang.

I couldn't claim the idea as my own, because I actually borrowed it from my cousin-in-law Cuzzo who taught me the rules of the heroin game. He kept one phone for hustling purposes and one for personal use, and he never gave his customers his personal number or vice versa.

It made complete sense to me at the time, so when I decided to give up the job hunt and get back to the street work I adopted its practice to my hustle. My only problem was that I peddled a variety of products, so instead of putting them all together, to keep it simple for me I just bought a new phone every time I added another product to my repertoire.

"Because I can babe." I stated to her sarcastically as I put my shoes on and my phone began to sing again "Hey now".

"I'm getting off at Goodfellow right now, which way again?" the caller questioned.

"Buck a right, two lights, first right, and I'll be waiting on you." I instructed.

"What?" The caller responded clearly confused.

"I said make a right, pass two stop lights, make the first right, and I'll be waiting on you." I explained before ending the call.

I need to stop selling this shit" I thought to myself as I filled my pockets with everything that I thought I might need while I was out and about: money, phones, cigarettes, lighter, keys, and an ID.

I always left my goodie bag and the pistol that accompanied it by the front door to ensure that I would never leave home without them. The bag promised that I could fulfill any order that got called in, and the gun promised my protection for the proceeds. It was an unwritten rule that every hustler that I knew followed to a tee. I had actually seen what happened to someone that had broke it one too many times, and I had no intentions of suffering his fate.

"I'd rather have it and not need it, than to need it and not have it." I thought to myself as I ran out of the house and jumped in my car.

I could feel my personal phone vibrating in my pocket as I pulled off, but I paid no mind. There was a couple of dollars waiting on me just a few blocks away, and that was the only thing other than my surroundings that had my attention. Safety and security first, get money second.

By the time I made it to the place that I had instructed my customer to go, I had circled the area twice to make sure that the police were not hanging out in the neighborhood. I had neglected this practice one time being lazy and ended up in a high speed chase that could have been avoided.

Fifty dollars richer and at least ten blocks away from my illicit transaction, I took the time to fish my personal phone out of my pocket to check it. It showed that I had one unread text message, but before I could see who it was from, my other phone that happened to be sitting in my lap began to sing to me again.

The thought crossed my mind to respond to the message before answering the money call, but followed the next thought instead. "Hey now. Where you at?"

For the next few hours my business phone wouldn't stop singing to me, and I didn't have a problem with it at all because money moved me. Each call kept me in motion and I made sure that I stayed out of my own neighborhood while I worked. My uncle used to tell me to "never shit in my own back yard" when I was younger, but it took for me to start selling drugs to understand exactly what it was that he was talking about. He told me all sorts of things that I will never forget, and it never ceased to amaze me how each one of them related to hustling in one way or another.

When my phone stopped singing to me, I finally took a few minutes to deal with my personal phone.

It seemed like everybody that I knew was trying to get in contact with me in one way or another and I had missed them all. Honestly I had ignored my personal line for my business line because on my long list of priorities the one that pays comes first. Plus, I had no real intentions or interest in celebrating my birthday anyway. The death of my uncle had truly ruined the day that I was born for me, and there was nothing that could be done to change it."Yesterday is gone, and tomorrow will never come." I thought to myself as I weaved in and out of traffic making my way back towards my house. When I walked out of the front door the sun was out but in full force now it was setting.

   The last customer that I had bumped into was only ten dollars short of purchasing the last of what my goodie bag had to offer so I gave her the couple of extras and wished her a happy birthday before taking her money and speeding off.

   Always aware of my surroundings and the things that were going on around me at all times. I took note of every vehicle that I thought could be an undercover cop because of The Jump Out, The Dick, and The Fed Boys had gotten smarter and switched from driving marked to unmarked cars. They had almost caught me slipping on more than one occasion, but almost didn't count.

   A few blocks from my house something out of the corner of my eye caught my attention. Turning my head in that direction I noticed a car that I had seen a few times while I was out and about. I paid it no mind the first couple of times I seen it, but there was something about this time that was different. Something deep inside of me made me focus on it even though I couldn't see who was actually inside of it because of the tint.

   The thought crossed my mind to continue going where I was headed but I went with my gut. Passing up the street that led to my house I switched from the inside to the turning lane. I made the first right turn I came to while keeping the car in question in my rear view mirror.

After I turned the corner I noticed that the car followed suit. That really got my attention and made me just a tad bit nervous. But not one to jump to conclusions even though my occupation encouraged paranoia, I still put just a little bit of distance between me and that car.

"I wonder who the fuck that it?" I asked myself as I quickly made the next left. But before I could begin to come up with an answer to my question, all was explained to me with the simple gesture as the red, white, and blue lights partially illuminated the inside of my car through the tint on my back windows.

Chapter Two

"Where the Charger at Day?" Chris questioned as he walked into the waiting room of his tint/car wash/detail shop.

"I don't know." I answered.

"What do you mean you don't know?" He laughed. "What happened to it?"

"Like I said bro, I don't know bro, I don't know where that damn car at. The last time I seen that motherfucker 'Them People' was trying to stop it while I caught my cut." I explained.

"That's bullshit." He commented as he looked at the floor and shook his head.

"It's easier to get a car out of the impound lot than it is to get a nigga out of jail." My uncle used to say every time the police got behind him while he was driving. And even though he was too old to practice what he preached, I did every time the status quo fit the situation.

"So what can I do for you today" He questioned.

"I need 5% tint all the way around" I explained as I handed him the keys to the up to date Impala I was now driving.

"Windshield too? He paused to take the keys. "Where you keep getting these cars from anyway?"

"Rental cometh, rental goeth. And I already said all the way around." I answered.

Since I started back hustling I had been in more high speed car chases than I cared to think about because they came right along with the lifestyle. It was that or go to jail and after my extended stay the first time around I had made up my mind that I would not be going back without at least a chase.

It took Chris a little less than an hour to handle any car that I brought to him, but I never stuck around to watch the process. His shop sat right on the corner of Natural Bridge Ave and Fair and in my honest opinion it was a death trap. There were too many things that needed to be watched out for or guarded against to sit there and wait.

If it wasn't the whatever district police, The Jump Out Boys, or any of the other numerous law enforcement agencies that patrolled the area. It was the Jack Boys or one of the numerous Blood or Cript gangs that lurked in that part of St. Louis.

I'd had a run-in with all of them at one point in my life of running the streets and though I had made it out of each one of them in one piece, I was in no rush to relive those experiences. They had all cost me something or another that I really didn't want to part with at the time, but I learned that nothing is free in the street game so I charged every loss that I endured to the game that I chose to play and continued forward.

"Call me when you finished." I instructed him as I exited the shop and took off walking.

Trying to decide what I wanted to do for an hour while I waited on my car, by the time I made up my mind I was two blocks away from the shop inside of the local liquor store. Chris had asked me about where my cars were coming from, and as I looked at the Moet bottles behind the counter, she crossed my mind.

Moet's government name was Monica and she was average all the way around the board. Average height, weight, and even skin color. The only things about Monica that were not average were her nickname and the fact that she worked for Avis Rental Care Company.

Not only did she work for them, she was actually the manager of her branch. And being the manager afforded her certain privileges that I took full advantage of. Along with her position she was also something like a genius with a computer and knew everything that there was to know about her job, including how to rent cars to me in other people's names.

I wondered how she was able to pull that off without getting caught, so I pillow talked her out of the information. Somehow she kept the car rented out in the name of the last person that used it and just let me continue to pay for the car in cash. The best part about it was that no matter what I did with or in the car the trail never led back to her.

The Charger that I had jumped out of on my birthday cost one of her employees his job, but the decision came down from someone higher up in the company. It also cost me an average night at Moet's loft downtown. She tried her best to outlast me, but almost an hour into our quality time together she had given up, in, and out.

"I need to find my way downtown tonight" I thought to myself as I ordered and paid for a pack of cigarettes, some gum, and a lighter.

Moet's favorite past time was texting, so after packing my squares, popping the pack, and firing one up, I took a few minutes to send her a very detailed note about what I wanted to do to her when she got off work, if she'd let me. I didn't give her the exact order in which I planned to accomplish my goal, I just made sure that she got all of the facts in the most sexually explicit words that I could come up with off the top of my head.

Almost two blocks from the liquor store I had to laugh to myself as I looked at her response to my explicit text. "That depends on the order you plan to do that."

"This lady really think she know me." I thought to myself as I continued my stroll in the opposite direction of the tint shop, but before I could respond to her response my other phone started singing to me.

I had directed the last four people that wanted to see me to meet me somewhere near Natural Bridge and Newstead before I pulled up to drop my car off at the tint shop, and I was only a block away when the first one of them called me back- "Hey now".

It worked out just like I wanted it to in the end, because by the time I finally handled all four of the transactions that I expected and two others that came along the way, I was only a half a block away from the tint shop when Chris called to inform me that my car was ready to be picked up. I hadn't planned to walk around conducting business the whole hour he was working on my car, but I preferred to be in motion while I worked even if it wasn't in a car.

"This motherfucker look like something them people might be in." Chris laughed as he tossed me the keys and motioned me inside of the garage.

"You ain't bullshitting." I responded as I walked around and checked out his work. "What's the ticket?" I questioned when I finished looking it over.

"Give me a hundred fifty." He answered.

I had planned to haggle over the price for a few minutes using the imperfections that I had found during my once over inspection as points of reference in my argument. But before I could get my process started my business phone decided to interrupt our conversation- "Hey now".

The caller's order more than covered the hundred and fifty dollars that he was charging me for the work, so I paid without saying a word in contention and got in the car. He must have known that my call saved him from an argument that would have probably saved me at least thirty dollars or more, because as I pulled out of the garage he showed me his phone along with my money then laughed before putting both of them in his pockets.

The sight made me want to stop and talk him out of some of my money, but as I turned around to park in front of the shop the sight of a marked St. Louis City police car riding down the street changed my mind instantly. Getting off of his parking lot became more important to me than my money was, so I kept my thought to myself and just made a mental note to get a double discount the next time that we did business.

Exiting the lot I did what I always do when I seen anything that looked like it could be the law. I went in the opposite direction. There were certain rules and regulations that went with driving and the police, and I tried my very best to follow them all to a tee. When I couldn't the car usually stayed at the scene while I followed another set of rules and regulations that concerned running for my life.

"I really need to stop selling this shit." I thought to myself as I pushed the two hundred and forty-five dollars into my pocket. It was supposed to be an even two fifty, but my customers usually exaggerated what they had for me on an average between five to ten dollars in search of a better deal.

At one point it got so bad that I changed my packaging procedure to increase my profit without increasing the price or decreasing the quality. I received several complaints behind it, but I responded to each one of them with the wonderful words of wisdom that I had committed to my memory years before. "You get what you pay for. Come short get shorted." My Uncle Percy used to say every time he did half the work for half the pay.

When things got better as far as the truth in sales went, I still employed the same tactic for a few extra days just to see what I had been missing and it amazed me. What I thought was only a few twos turned out to be a couple of fiftys and hundreds. I couldn't get mad at anybody but myself for taking the shorts, so after I got enough of my money back from the streets, I went back to my normal business practices.

Another text from Moet caught my attention and almost caused me to lose control of my car as I concentrated more on the screen of my phone than I did the road.

"Oh shit!" I screamed as I looked up just in time to keep from running into the back of the car in front of me. Moet's most intimate possession looked almost edible in the photo message she sent to me, and I couldn't keep my eyes off of it. I had seen it more times than I could count or remember, but every time she sent it to me through the mail it looked just a little bit better than usual.

When I was certain that I wasn't being followed, I took a few seconds to save the picture to my photo gallery of my phone. The bag that I had left home with that morning was almost empty, and that wasn't ever a good thing for business. So after I got Moet out of my lower mind, I made my way back home to put together another bag of goodies for the streets.

Since my Mr. Coffee blender did most of the work for one, and the stove did most of the work for the other, I was in and out of the house and back in traffic in just over an hour. My two business lines sung the same song all day and I did my very best to dance to their rhythm until I had no more moves to make.

At which time the calls and texts went out to replenish my inventory, but they were both answered with the "hurry up and wait" response that I'd quickly grown accustomed to. The thought crossed my mind to place an order with a different store, but I didn't act on it. I had made the mistake of shopping at different retail stores and it cost me several of my favorite customers. I ended up getting most of them back, but the ones that I didn't taught me a very valuable lesson about being in a rush to get back to work.

My cousin called it "killing the phone," and I completely agreed with the term. Because one day it would ring non-stop, and the next it wouldn't ring at all. I had suffered that death and been resurrected by hard hustling and word of mouth from the streets, but I refused to press my luck. I had seen several people that I associated with never bounce back, and I didn't want to be in their situation or anything close to it if I could help it.

"Can't miss a call I never catch." I told myself before turning off both of my business lines and tossing them into the cup holder in the center console.

My personal phone always had something going on with it because of the numerous social networks that I belonged to, so when I ran out of money to chase after, women became the next best substitute. Facebook, Twitter, and Instagram were confusing to me at first, but once I got the hang of them I was truly a natural. And even though I preferred to meet women face-to-face, I was not opposed to starting a cyber relationship as long as it got physical before it got emotional.

Closer to downtown than I was to home when Moet texted me that she was getting off of work, I made my way towards her loft. She lived a couple of blocks away from the club Lola, so I stopped there and had a drink to kill a few minutes as I waited on her to join me.

Lola's catered to a mixed crowd of street and working class people so I fit right in. It was also Moet's first stop after having a hard day at the office, so I was also something like a regular in the place because of all the times I met her there to pay for drinks or talk her into not quitting her job.

"I wonder what's taking Moet so long to pull up." I asked myself as I nursed my second drink, but the question came and went when an extremely attractive woman stopped right next to me at the bar and ordered a drink.

She was almost my height, light skinned, with long jet black hair. The fact that she was plus sized didn't bother me at all when I looked into her ocean blue eyes.

"Your drink is on me pretty lady." I informed her as I motioned to the bartender to put it on my tab. All I want in return is an honest answer to three questions."

"You gonna buy me a drink if I answer three questions, huh?" She replied with just a hint of suspicion in her voice.

"That's right." I answered lost in her eyes.

"Ok." She paused as she returned my stare. "Shoot."

"Those your eyes?" I questioned.

"Yes." She responded.

"Do you live in St. Louis?' I probed.

"Yes." She replied.

And what is your name?" I asked.

"Layla." She answered.

I had several other questions that I wanted to know the answers to, but I kept them to myself. The fact that Moet could walk up at any second was not far from the front of my mind, and I didn't want her to cause a scene or vice versa.

"I give you three questions and those were the best ones you could come up with?" She questioned me when I returned to nursing my drink.

"They told me everything that I really wanted to know at this point in my life." I explained.

"And what was that, if you don't mind me asking." She asked as if she didn't believe me.

"They told me that your beautiful eyes are real, I will see you again, and most importantly what to call you when I do." I paused long enough to pull more than enough money out of my pocket to cover my tab and toss it on the bar. "Now if you will excuse me. Enjoy your drink and your night. Until we meet again." I finished then walked away leaving her standing at the bar as I made my way towards the door Moet had just walked through.

Chapter Three

My uncle taught me the five Ps "proper preparation prevents poor performance", so I could do my very best in every situation that I got myself into. He also taught me that "when the mission changes unexpectedly never panic, always improvise," and that advice had helped me get through the rest. It was also the only reason I found myself at my cousin's front door.

"Cuzzo you got some dorman and baking soda?" I questioned him as soon as he opened the door.

"No what's up, no what's popping, not even a hi or hello? Nigga you rude as a motherfucker." He responded as if insulted.

"If you cry, then what the babies gonna do?" I shot back as I pushed my way passed him through the crack in the door. "And that didn't answer my first question pimp, you got some dorman and baking soda?"

"Dorman with the kit, Arm and Hammer in the fridge, and the Boy Wonder already in the kitchen." He answered from behind me as I took the steps by twos and threes headed upstairs.

Cuzzo lived in a two family flat right off of the corner of Euclid and Labadie in the heart of the city. The location didn't make sense to me when I helped him move in, and it was one of the main reasons I rarely visited afterward. He also figured in his mind that living on the second floor was safer than the first in regards to dealing with an outside threat, but I didn't share his sentiment on that either. In my mind, living on the second floor only made the ground that much farther away if leaving in a hurry became necessary.

That argument was probably the reason he more tolerated than loved me, but I didn't care at all. I had read in a book while on my long vacation, that when it comes to love and fear that it was better to be feared than loved anyway because it lasted longer.

"Where you car at Boy Wonder?" I questioned as I walked into the kitchen.

"I'm wit Skinny fat ass, but that nigga just shook to go bump into some of his good geeks." He answered.

My cousin might have taught me the rules and regulations of the heroin hustle, but the Boy Wonder showed me the true ins and outs. He was actually the reason I even wanted to learn about it, because he made it look so easy. It was like he was a model for the game. He walked, talked, dressed, and acted the part to perfection, and the fact that he was not even old enough to purchase liquor legally didn't mean a thing.

"Just like old times huh?" I commented as I took my place next to him to work on mixing up my package.

"Yeah, ain't it?" He laughed. "But now you doing you and from what I hear from the streets yo lil thing is picking up nicely."

"You taught me well sensei." I paused to bow.

"Where my bow at nigga?" Cuzzo questioned as he stood in the kitchen doorway staring at us.

The thought crossed my mind to say something completely uncalled for in response, but I bit my tongue instead. It seemed like déjà vu to me for some odd reason, and those moments always caused me to pause until I could figure out the when, where, and why of the situation.

Leave that nigga alone Day." The Boy Wonder advised me as he looked at the sign that hung above the kitchen door. "No losing at home and that include arguments." "You remember what happened the last time we was right here doing the same shit we doing now?"

"Yeah I remember bro. That nigga put me out for telling the truth. And if my memory serves me correctly, he put yo ass out for laughing at him." I paused to take in the scene. "I was just thinking to myself that this situation seemed so familiar to me."

"Good cause my daughter momma got the truck, my son momma got the car, I don't know when Skinny coming back, and I don't like this neighborhood." He explained before giving in to his laughter.

I couldn't contain my own giggle either when the thought popped into my head that the incident that we were talking about actually started out as a conversation with my cousin about his neighborhood and quickly escalated into an argument.

"Say one more word about where I live and I'm gonna put both of y'all asses out of here." Cuzzo threatened as he walked out of the kitchen being followed by our laughter.

Putting my package together with the help of the Boy Wonder took less than fifteen minutes and that worked out perfectly for me, because as soon as the mess was cleaned up and everything put back into its proper place my phone started to sing to me "Hey now".

I really didn't have anything special planned for the day before stopping at my cousin's house, so instead of leaving to chase my phone, I decided to direct all of my calls to somewhere close to where I was opposed to catching them in traffic. Skinny owed me some money for a bet we made on a baseball game, and since he had to come back to get the Boy Wonder, I planned to get it from him. He was the hardest person in the world to run into when he owed you money, but the easiest person to find when you owed him. Something about that didn't sit right with me, but I pushed it from my mind as my phone started to sing "Hey now".

All three of my customers came and went like clockwork as me and the Boy Wonder walked to the corner store that sat right across the street from Cuzzo's apartment. He wanted something to drink other than the unlimited supply of water that Cuzzo had to offer, and I was in complete agreement. I also wanted a couple of blunts because my last customer gave me a nice size bag of marijuana as a substitute for the few dollars that he was short on his purchase.

By the time we made it back from our store run I noticed that Shoota's van was parked right behind my car. He was also on my list of people that owed me money for some reason or another, and I had been looking to run into him for the last couple of weeks also, but it had not worked out anywhere like I wanted it to.

"This might be a good day." I thought to myself as I collected my money, exchanged greetings with Shoota, and rolled up my weed.

"Is that Reggie I smell my nigga?" Skinny questioned with a hint of disdain in his voice as he walked into the room.

"Are you a fat nigga named Skinny?" I responded as always when he asked me a question that didn't make sense to me.

"If that's the case bro." He paused just long enough to pull a few twenty dollar bills out of his pocket. "I will pay you to put that bullshit out." He offered as he tossed the bills on the table in front of me.

"Don't do him like that Skinny." Cuzzo instigated as he walked into the room behind him. "He been outta the loop for a few minutes with that bit he did in the joint and the one he caught when he came home and married that lady." He laughed.

"Don't mention that lady." I cut in. "That skeleton stays in the back of the closet.

"You right bro." Shoota jumped in. "Plus it ain't shit wrong with a little Reggie in the morning." He explained as he took the blunt from my hand and took a couple of puffs. "It's just once you turn up you have to stay that way for the rest of the day." He finished as he exhaled the smoke.

"I don't give a fuck what you say Shoota." Skinny responded as he began to pat his pockets in search of something. "It's loud or nothing with me. Motherfuck some Reggie." He paused to pullout a sandwich bag from his pocket. "Do I need to remind you of your first loud experience?" He stopped to smell the bag. "Cause if I ain't mistaken, I almost didn't make it out of that one alive." He finished as him and Cuzzo laughed as they remembered the story.

"Don't nobody wanna hear that shit." The Boy Wonder cut in. "That's another skeleton for the back of the closet my nigga, just fire that shit up before Cuzzo put us out." He finished as all of us except Cuzzo laughed.

Smoking weed was not really my thing though I indulged every now and then. I basically figured that all marijuana was the same in one way or another, and due to the fact that it took extremely large amounts of it to turn a small profit on the hustling end, I never put too much thought in to it. I had heard about Kush from being around the fellows, but after tasting the flavor and feeling the immediate effects that came with the high, thoughts of money began to come to me from out of nowhere.

"Skinny where the fuck you are getting this loud shit from?" I questioned after I got my thoughts all the way back together.

"The Boy Wonder's dude Miser." He smiled showing all ten of his gold teeth. "And he keeps that gas."

"What is gas Skinny?" I paused to puff then pass.

"The weed nigga." He laughed. It goes by so many different names. Loud, gas, thrax, just to name a few. All I really know is that I blow at least a dollar a day smoking this shit." He explained.

"Well if that's the case would you please pay me them couple of dollars you owe me for that Cardinals- Cubs game we bet on before you spend it?" I suggested to him before turning towards the Boy Wonder. "Can you get me and your dude in the same room?"

"Miser is my cousin not one of my dudes." The Boy Wonder explained. "So yeah just let me know when you ready. As a matter of fact I'll just text you his number and you set it up yourself.

"What you got up your sleeve Day?" Skinny questioned as he handed me the money that he owned me.

"Daniel-son probably looking for a new master." Cuzzo chimed in before I could respond.

The thought of the perfect retort to Cuzzo's sarcastic comment crossed my mind, but before I could let it roll off of my tongue I was pleasantly interrupted by my phone singing to me. The words said kind of what I wanted to say, so I just sang along with it as I made my way towards the front door. "And I understand hate, but I can't comprehend the hatin/ When you can use that energy to go and get some paper/ Hey now."

Chapter Four

As I pulled up in front of the Best Steak House, a thousand and one different thoughts were running through my mind. The night before hadn't gone anywhere close to the well laid plan that I had set up for myself, but I still couldn't complain. I wanted to more than I really wanted to anything else, but that didn't make dollars and anything other than that didn't make sense.

"It took you long enough to pull up nigga. I was just about to shake". Miser informed me as he held the door to the restaurant open for me.

"My fault dirty, I had two sells to catch, and one of them got lost." I explained.

The thought crossed my mind to fill him in on the series of very unfortunate events that had filled the previous 16 hours of my life, but I decided against it and pushed the thought from my mind. My trials and tribulations were just that, and nothing that I had to say would change the fact that they happened or the way that they were eventually overcome. They were my issues, and I planned to keep it that way.

"Since I was late bro, lunch is on me." I offered as we stood in line to place our orders.

"You my type of nigga Day, but don't worry about it. I got this one covered for more than one reason." He paused.

By the time we got drinks and sat at a table in the back of the building facing the front door, the smell and sight of my steak, chicken, and French fries had my complete attention. I knew that I was hungry before I got there, but with the food sitting right in front of me, my hunger raised up to a level that I hadn't known it could get to.

"I know you ain't got all day to be bullshitting with me, so let me get to the point." I paused to enjoy a nice sized portion of my steak. "I gotta do something different with my life, so if you don't mind I would love for you to give me the 4-1-1 on the loud hustle you got going on."

"It ain't no different than what you already got going on. The only real difference is the consequences that come with the act." He explained.

The pros and cons of the products that I was dealing with were extreme on both ends. The money came in hand over fist as long as the quality was right, but the punishment for being caught with those products cost at least what they brought in if not more. Also the laws concerning drugs and their possession changed several times while I was on my extended vacation due to the system, and with at least one strike against me, the consequences and cost doubled.

"Loud is the new crack dirty." Miser explained between bites of his food. "Plus on top of that anything under 35 grams is considered a misdemeanor."

"Now you talking my language. What do I really need to know?" I questioned.

As Miser explained to me the ins and outs of his occupation, he was interrupted by his phone ringing. After taking the call and giving the caller his location, he continued explaining and eating.

"So let me get this straight, dirty, it basically boils down to what you have and who you know." I rephrased.

"That's it pimp. If you got loud it's gonna sell itself just like any other drug. And the better it is, the faster it's gonna sell." He paused to answer his phone. "Now if you'll excuse me, I got to get back to chasing that paper." He finished before getting up and leaving me to my meal.

"Now that I completely understand." I said to myself as I finished eating my food. I had the same thought on my mind, but I was in no rush to get back to answering my phone.

The meeting with Miser had given me a lot to think over, and I didn't have anything better to do with my time. An old head had told me that the best place to think was behind the wheel of a car, and as I cruised through the city streets seeing the sights, I couldn't agree with him more.

A thousand things ran through my mind during my drive, but they all revolved around the same things (what I had, and who I knew).

Those two things were the negatives and positives of my situation, and as I processed the simpleness of it, the multiple pieces of the puzzle began to come together. The picture wasn't as clear to me as I might have wanted it to be, but I knew that the more thought that I put into it, the more I would see. The problem was what I had, the solution was probably in who I knew, but I had so many other things on mind at that moment that it wasn't coming together like I wanted it to. Plus my phone had started back singing to me, and that took priority over my plans.

"A bird in the hand beats two in the bush." I thought to myself as I answered the phone "Hey now".

Where's the biz bro? Where you at in the world?" Dizel questioned.

"I'm skating down Grand. I got a couple of good geeks waiting on me to pull up. What's shaking?" I responded.

"I heard about your misadventure last night. When you get the chance dirty, pull up on me." He stated.

"Where you at bro?" I questioned.

"I'm at the trap house." He answered.

"Give me a few minutes." I paused to check my mirrors. "I got you covered. One." I finished before ending the call and tossing the phone back on the seat next to me.

Knowing that the place that I had told my customers to meet me at was a hot spot as far as the local law enforcement were concerned didn't bother me at all, but I still took the proper precautions before pulling up to make the transaction. 'Better safe than sorry' was a statement that I lived by to a degree in my recreational life, but always when hustling. The money meant nothing if I wasn't alive or free to do anything meaningful or meaningless with it.

My two stops worked out just like they were supposed to, and I was back in traffic in less than two minutes. The four hundred dollars that I picked up put me right where I wanted to be money wise for the day, but since my phone continued to ring, I continued to answer it. Dizal's trap house was only a few minutes down the highway from where I happened to be, so I just directed my customers in that direction so I could kill two birds with one stone. I wasn't sure about how he feels about me running traffic to his house, so instead I just served them around the corner from the house before I pulled up to see what he wanted.

"I wonder what this nigga want?" I thought to myself as I knocked on the back door.

"Who is it?" A voice questioned from the other side of the reinforced steel door.

"Day" I answered.

When the door opened up it didn't surprise me at all that there was a youngster on the other side armed with a Glock 23 fitted with an extender clip.

"Where Dizal at?" I inquired as I walked into the house.

"He in the front room cuz." He answered as he pointed his gun towards the front of the house.

The thought crossed my mind to ask the youngster his name, but it came and went just as fast because Dizal had more young soldiers on his payroll than I could possibly keep track of even if I wanted to.

"What's the biz bro?" I questioned as I walked into the front room.

"You tell me." Dizal answered as he sat on the couch with his feet propped up on the living room table.

"What you talking about dirty?" I paused as I sat on the other end of the couch. "Who all here?"

"Just me and Lil Cuz, Banga, CB, Ugly Cuz, and GLoc just left. But fuck that. What the fuck happened last night?" He questioned.

"Long or short version?" I asked.

"Long.. And please don't leave out the part you know that I really wanna hear." He answered.

"What's that bro?" I questioned even though I knew exactly what it was that he was talking about.

"The part about how you still amongst the living my nigga." He paused as he passed me the blunt he was smoking. "I told you that I heard about what happened. I just would love to hear yo side of the story."

I had been trying to let the thoughts about what happened to me the night before go, but I was starting to realize that from Dizal's call to the multiple text messages that I kept trying to ignore on my personal phone, that letting it go was actually going to be a lost cause. Everybody seemed to want to know what happened, so I decided to tell Dizal then deal with my phone situations.

"Last night I ended up at the strip club because Diosa tick ass was on my mind something heavy. Something told me before I walked into the Pink Slip that I should have just went home, but I didn't listen. I followed my first mind thought and everything was alright for the first hour or so. I had a couple of drinks, smoked a blunt or two, and tricked off a few dollars to some of the fresh meat that I hadn't seen while I waited on Diosa to hit the stage, but that's when shit went south on me." I paused as I passed him his blunt back. "Diosa hit the stage to do what she do, and I was front row center like I always am.

"That's cause you a trick Day." Dizal cut it.

Don't judge me bro. It ain't tricking if she yo bitch." I responded in my defense. "So I go wit maybe three hundred in ones so I can make it rain on the bitch, but it's two or three other niggas in the club thinking the exact same thought. So one thing lead to another, and somehow I must have offended the niggas cause they started talking reckless to me and giving me that look that I'm scared to death of.

I ain't really tripping off of the niggas though, but the talk did get my attention. You already know I'm scary as that one that, and before you ask, yes I am strapped. So instead of leaving and letting them have their fun and harsh words in my direction. I ended up getting another thousand in ones and really showing off. Plus I already knew that I was going to get most if not all of my money back after Diosa got off work, so I made it shake.

The niggas on the other hand refused to be outdone though, so we went back and forth tipping. The only problem for them was Diosa my bitch." I paused to hit the blunt again. "So after they went broke I got all the love that they thought was suppose to come they way, and that didn't sit right with them. So more talk, more dirty looks.

By then I was ready to leave anyway, and that's when I seen that look that really scares me again."

"That's fine and dandy." He cut in. "What happened after that? And fuck the long version, give it to me short and sweet."

"You should have said that shit in the first place." I paused as I passed the blunt back. "To make a long story short, after I left the club, them clown ass niggas followed me, tried to box me in, shot up my car, and found out the hard way that not only do I shoot back, but also that I had way more shots than they did. But that's the type of shit that happens to me.

"But on another note, who do you know got a line on that good loud?" I questioned.

Chapter Five

"Hyatt Regional. Layla speaking, how may I direct your call?" Layla questioned after answering the phone.

"Actually you can't direct my call, because I'm calling to speak directly to you." I answered.

"Who is this?" She asked with a hint of suspicion in her voice.

"That's a damn good question." I paused to get my thoughts all the way together. "My name is Day."

I don't know anyone named Day. But since you must know me Day, what do you want? She questioned.

You. I want you. And before you respond to that please think carefully about what your next question will be. I asked you three and I have already answered one of yours." I explained.

The phone went silent for what seemed like forever and for a split second I actually thought she had hung up on me. Calling her at work wasn't the first plan of action that I had come up with after Moet had given me a few very useful pieces of information, but nothing else I had come up with had worked out anywhere close to how I wanted it to. The couple of times I had stopped by in person hoping to run into her accidentally on purpose were a waste of time, and my occupation made waiting for her to get off work a bad idea that I refused to pursue.

"How did you find me?" She questioned breaking me from my thought.

"Are you sure that's the question you want me to answer?" I responded.

"Yep. I'm positive. How did you find me?" She repeated.

The thought crossed my mind to make up some type of high powered lie that would make the truth seem so dull in comparison, but lying wasn't my style. One of my favorite sayings is "I don't lie for free", and since there was no money involved in our conversation I decided to stick with the truth.

"I have a very close friend named Moet who told me who you were, where you worked, and what days I could probably catch you at the club." I explained.

When I finished there was another pause in the conversation, which I later found out was her putting me on hold to answer another line. When she spoke again she gave me her personal phone number, what time she wanted me to call, and wished me a blessed day. I wanted to say something in response, but before

I could I found out that after her last word she actually did hang up on me.

"I like that." I said to myself as I programmed her number into my phone, and made a mental note of what time she told me to call her.

My business line had rung a few times while I was talking to her, but I paid it no mind. From past experience I knew that whoever had called me would call back, and just as I thought about that fact it started singing to me "Hey now".

Back in the day it was almost unheard of to hustle on the move, but with time comes changes. Setting up shop in one place has more cons than pros when it comes to accessibility, and that is always bad for business. I had read in a book somewhere that "the more people you can reach, the more money you can make". At the time it sounded silly to me, but after putting that theory to the test with actual practice, my mind was forever changed on the subject.

There are so many rules and regulations that come with hustling that at times they are almost hare to keep track of. Don't get high on your own supply. Never keep the money and the product in the same place. Keep your friends close and your enemies closer.

And the list goes on and on, but there is one that makes the most sense to me, and I follow it to the letter. It's extremely hard to hit a moving target, and that's where I am as long as my business is mobile.

By the time my business line decided that it wanted to slow down, it was ten minutes passed the time that I was supposed to call Layla back, and she let me know about it the first ten minutes of our conversation. I couldn't be mad about it though because punctuality is a quality that I find extremely sexy in a woman. She felt the same way about men, and I made sure that I made a mental note about it before I changed the direction of our conversation towards a few things that I really wanted to know.

No kids, job, car, apartment, and my personal favorite- she was into women also. Her stats lined up perfect with the team that I was putting together, and I let it be known.

She found it funny that I didn't ask and wasn't concerned about if she was seeing anybody, but I paid it no mind. That subject could only place an obstacle in front of me that I would need to overcome, and that was against my motto for dealing with women; "Never open a door for another nigga to walk through".

After giving her my stats (no kids, multiple hustles, several cars (one of which happened to be in the shop), house, and a couple of female friends, she ended the call so she could get ready for a night out at the clubs. My business line must have known that I was back open for business, because as soon as our call ended, it started singing "Hey now".

An old head once told me that it's easy to lose track of time when money is involved", and I couldn't agree with him more, because by the time I made it back home after an uneventful day and night of following where my phone led me, the sun was coming back up. And though I hadn't planned on being out all night, it didn't matter because I didn't have anything else planned.

Sitting in my driveway with the car still running and the music turned down low, I thumbed through the check, smoked a blunt, and watched the sun rise.

In my 30 something odd years on the earth, I never really took the time out to enjoy the beginning of a new day. My momma used to always use the quote "as beautiful as a sun rise" to describe things that she thought were pretty, and I never understood why. But after witnessing one for myself without any distractions, I had to admit that momma was still 100 for 100 on everything she had ever told me.

"This might be an alright day." I thought to myself as I got out of the car, chirped the alarm, and walked across my front yard.

I was almost at my front door when my personal phone started ringing, and my thought for an alright day went right out the window. I knew exactly who it was, and what she wanted before I even looked at the phone, but it didn't stop me from praying that I was wrong. But as usual, I wasn't.

"Hey now Moet babe, what's shaking this early in the morning?" I questioned after answering the phone.

"You ain't shit Day!: She responded.

"What are you talking about babe?" I paused to open my front door and step inside of the house. "What I do now?"

"Where are you Day?" She questioned with anger in her tone.

"Why?" I answered just to check the level of her anger.

"Why?" I answered as I locked the front door and made my way towards the kitchen for something to drink.

"Don't worry about it Day. I know now." She paused for effect. "When you get home?"

The thought crossed my mind to ask why, but it left just as fast as I reopened the front door and looked out as I ended our phone call.

"This should be interesting." I said to myself as Moet got out of her car and gave me a look that could have probably started a fight. I had seen it before on a couple of previous occasions, and after the night/morning I had already endured, I was in no mood to revisit the screaming, arguing, cussing, and sex that always followed that look. I was tired from my all-nighter and I knew that I only had enough energy left to do one or the other, so as soon as she walked through the door I let it be known.

"What you mean one or the other." She questioned as she stood toe to toe with me.

"Babe I been up all night chasing my phone, so if you came over here to fight and fuck baby, pick one cause I'm going to sleep on the other." I explained.

"You got me fucked up Day." She began as she unbuttoned her pants and kicked off her shoes. "This is not over."

"Yes it is." I mumbled under my breath as I followed her lead and started taking off my clothes.

Usually I'm something like a neat freak, but after my night the trail of clothes leading from the living room to my bedroom didn't bother me at all. To be completely honest, it was kind of sexy. The only thing that threw it off was the fact that Moet would not stop mumbling under her breath how she was feeling about the situation, but I paid her no mind. I had the perfect solution for that problem, and I put it into effect as soon as we got into the bed by putting my dick in her mouth. I can't say if it was the fact that I was super tired, she was mad at me, or a weird combination of both, but for some odd reason as I laid back to enjoy both the silence and the head, I was truly surprised by the sensations that were running through my body. Moet's oral skills in my opinion were nothing to get excited over, but as she worked her way up and down the shaft of my dick, she was quickly changing my mind on the subject.

The thought crossed my mind to complement the job she was doing with her mouth, but I kept it to myself. I had a couple of other things on my mind that took precedence over sex, and no matter how much I tried to concentrate on what was in front of me, my thoughts kept returning to those. So much so that I was almost ready to fake a fall out so I wouldn't have to finish what she started, but before I could speak Moet stopped working me over.

"Day I know this ain't the right time to want to talk to you but I have something that I need to say." She paused as I shook my head in agreement. "I know I'm not the only bitch you fucking with and I'm cool with it. You always there when I need you and no matter what I ask you for somehow you always make it shake."

"We already know that babe." I cut in. Is there a point you tryin to make or are you just stating the obvious to throw me off as you set me up for the kill."

"I have a point I'm trying to make." She answered.

"Well what is it?" I questioned.

"The point I'm tryin to make is no matter what or who you do, I want you to promise me that I will never lose you." She explained as she stared right into my eyes.

Instead of responding to her statement, I just shook my head in agreement, but that wasn't enough. I had known her for longer than I could remember, and that did not work in my favor in serious situations because she knew me almost better than I knew myself. She knew that my promises meant more to me than anything else, and she would not settle for anything less.

"Day, promise." She demanded as her eyes began to fill with tears.

I had only seen her cry on one other occasion, and I was really not in the mood to revisit that scene. Several other things crossed my mind as I watched a tear leave her left eye and roll down her cheek. Every thought revolved around times that she held me down when I really needed her, and that was all I needed to know to make up my mind on the issue.

"If I promise will you go to sleep?" I questioned.

"Yes." She responded as another tear left her right eye.

"Ok Monica, I promise." I paused just long enough to pull her closer to me. "Now take yo ass to sleep."

Chapter Six

"Damn nigga, when you get out?" A voice called to me as I stood on my front porch lost in thought.

Several things crossed my mind as I processed the voice, and strangely none of them had a good ending for me, but instead of following my first mind to break for cover, I calmly turned in the direction of the voice prepared for the worst, but that wasn't the case. It turned out to be a childhood friend that I hadn't seen since I got locked up so many years before.

"What's shaking B, long time no see." I responded as I stepped off of the porch to meet him half way.

"Same bullshit just another day of it." He answered as we shook hands.

More than ten years had passed since our last conversation, but it didn't seem like it. It almost felt like I had just talked to him the day before due to the casualness, but almost didn't count. An old head had once told me that "almost counts in horseshoes and hand grenades", and though I never really understood where he was going with the examples, I completely understood the point he was trying to make.

"So what you got going on these days?" I questioned.

"What you know about that loud shit?" He asked.

The question caught me off guard for a split second because I just knew that it wasn't going to be that easy to find who I had been looking for since I had my sit down with Miser, but I played along expecting the same run around that I had been getting on the subject from every other person that I brought it up to.

"I know everything except where to get it at a hustler's price. Why?" I answered.

I figured that I was in for the same speech that I had heard from the last few old friends that I had happened to run into in the streets, but after the long drawn out spill about how far we went back, and how glad he was to see me free, he let me know that I could stop looking around because he had it. It sounded good at first, but after throwing the numbers back and forth, it started to sound even better. The only problem that I had with the whole situation was the fact that it was all talk.

After exchanging numbers and catching up on a few old times and things that I had missed while I was gone, he let me know that he would catch up with me after he got off to work. It was strange to hear that B had a real job because when we were youngsters running the streets, he would always tell me that he would never work for anybody other than himself, but with time comes changes. The thought crossed my mind to ask him about it, but I let the moment come and go. I had other more important matters to attend to, so we parted ways with the mutual understanding that we would finish our conversation at a later time.

   When I stepped back into the house the sound of my business line singing to me brought my thoughts back around to the business that I needed to handle. I found that I had at least ten missed calls from seven different people when I finally found the phone that happened to be in the last place that I thought it would be. I couldn't remember throwing it in the drawer next to my bed, but I could vaguely remember Latoya and her extremely thick friend Eri complaining about it being a distraction. I didn't share their opinion on the subject, but it was either them or the phone, and after looking over my choices for a few moments they won with me hands down.

   Looking over my call log of missed calls, I noticed that my cousin had called more than once. The thought crossed my mind to ignore his call, but I went against my better judgment and called him back.

"I knew I should have followed my first mind." I chastised myself after getting off the phone with him. It was always something when it came to dealing with him on any level, but for some odd reason I couldn't bring myself to turn him down. The definition of insanity is doing the same thing over and over again, expecting or looking for a different result, and that was exactly what I was doing every time I dealt with him. I couldn't count on my hands, toes, or any other body part for that matter how many times I was there when he needed me, but I knew the exact amount of times it worked out in my favor, because zero is an easy number to remember.

It took me a few minutes to digest the fact that I had actually agreed to let him come live with me. I completely understood his plight with not being able to get along with his live in girlfriend, but it boggled my mind why he was choosing to leave instead of her when he was supposedly paying all of the bills. That was probably another story that I had no interest in hearing, so I pushed it out of my mind, came to grips with my decision, then got my day started.

A few sells later, I found myself on the other side of the city with nothing planned, and nothing else better to do, so I called Layla to see what her lunch plans were. It surprised her to no end that I was interested in a lunch date, but I paid her no mind. We had played phone tag off and on since I called her job, and I was tiring of it rapidly. The thought had actually crossed my mind to give up my pursuit of her and find me something else to chase with my time, but luckily for the both of us nothing else more appealing had caught my attention.

I couldn't decide what I wanted to eat, so after throwing ideas back and forth, we both agreed that Hard Rock Cafe would work out perfectly for the both of us. She would still be downtown close to her job, and I could still answer my phone and run traffic through the parking lot. She didn't agree with my choice of occupation, but on the flip side of the coin, she really didn't object either, and that was all that I asked.

After the first drink and the food was delivered the subject of what I actually did to make my ends meet finally came up. Previous to that the explanation of I hustled was good enough to get me by, but I knew that wouldn't be good enough this time as she stared me down with her salt water blue eyes asking me for a straight answer.

My first two or three thoughts all revolved around coming as close to the truth as possible without actually doing so, but I couldn't bring myself to do it. I didn't even know why I wanted to in the first place because I wasn't ashamed of what I did or how I did it, so I took another sip of my drink as I put my words together in my mind.

"To be completely honest beautiful I'm a drug dealer." I explained as I returned her stare.

In the back of my mind I figured that our meal was over and that she was about to get up and leave, but her only response was to question why I hadn't or wouldn't do anything else with my life.

On more than one occasion I found myself on the receiving end of that type of question, so my answer was more than well rehearsed. It was also trial tested by more than one legal profession, and even they couldn't refute my logic.

"So you telling me that you sell drugs simply because the pros outweigh the cons for your situation?" She questioned after taking a few minutes to completely digest my answer.

"That's not what I said, but it's close enough to call it fair." I responded.

"You right Day. What you said was...That you do what you do because of the benefit/consequence ratio is in your favor as long as the proper precautions are taken." She paused to roll her eyes. "Would you care to elaborate?"

"Why certainly." I shot back with a hint of sarcasm in my tone before explaining how I came up with my insight and opinion on the subject.

Only being able to speak and think for myself, my situation to me was cut and dried to be what it was. Being that I had no children, no true family ties except for a few family members that I chose to deal with, and an attitude that bordered on the thin line between genius and insanity, I looked at life from a different angle than most people. The consequences and repercussions for my actions, occupation, and thought process boiled down to two things: death or jail. Being that I had experienced jail for more than a decade, and came to a true understanding that death cannot under any circumstances be avoided, the math always added up in my favor. Hustling afforded me the opportunity to experience my every whim without the delays and struggles that came with working for someone else.

My phone must have figured that we had been intertwined in that conversation long enough, because as soon as I finished with my explanation it started to sing to me. "Now that's what I call instant gratification." I laughed before answering the call.

After the directions were given, and the phone placed back on the table in its spot right within my reach, we finished lunch in almost complete silence. The only communication between us was being made via eye contact, but it wasn't a bad thing. I received at least four smiles and two winks before I excused myself from the table to step outside to handle business.

The thought actually crossed my mind to keep going after I caught my customer in the parking lot, but I pushed the thought from my mind. I wasn't sure how I would be able to accomplish my goal of getting to know all of Layla by leaving her to pay the check on our first lunch date, so I didn't.

"I'm surprised you came back." She commented as I sat back down at our table.

"What made you say that?" I questioned though she was not far from the truth.

"Because you left without paying the check, even though we were done eating." She paused to look at the check on the table.

"So I figured that you were gone, I was stuck with the bill, and I would never hear from you again. You know how niggas do it when you put them in uncomfortable situations."

"First off, I don't like niggas." I paused just long enough to pay the check. "Second, this was my idea so I got the bill covered. Third, I'm only uncomfortable in handcuffs, state grays, and prison cells. So if you don't wanna fuck with me then say that now, cause I meant what I said when you asked me what I wanted from you."

"And what was that? Please refresh my memory." She asked.

"You. I want you." I answered.

"We'll see about that." She paused to get up from the table. "I have to get back to work, so take the proper precautions and I'll call you later."

"I'm fucking the shit out of her the first chance I get." I said to myself as I watched her leave. Big girls were not usually my thing, but there was something about her that I found extremely sexy. I didn't know if it was her eyes, her high yellow complexion, he jazzy attitude, or the fact that she was bigger than me, but whatever it was I had made up my mind that I had to have her for as long as I could keep her around.

I didn't have any other plans for the day, so after leaving the restaurant I hit Unison Station to walk around the mall. There was something about new things that was almost therapeutic to me for some reason. On more than one occasion I had been referred to as a shopaholic and it didn't offend me at all. As a matter of fact I wore it as a badge of honor whenever something new came out and I was the first person I knew with it. That was one of the real perks that came with my occupation, and I truly enjoyed it whenever the opportunity presented itself.

Lost in thought as I browsed the racks at the Foot Locker looking for a shoe that I didn't already have that I might want, I almost missed my personal phone ringing. When I pulled it out, I noticed that what I thought was a call was only a text message from Layla thanking me for lunch, and apologizing for not having a little faith in me. The thought crossed my mind to respond to her text with a slick comment about how she could make it up to me, but before I could I received another text from her promising to make it up to me in one way or another.

After sending her back an Ok text in response, my business phone caught my attention and it always took precedence over my personal line. I almost didn't even answer it, but my greed go the better of me instantly; "Hey now".

I figured that the call was from one of my good geeks looking to increase my profit margin for the day, but when I heard B's voice it didn't bother me at all. I had actually forgotten all about that he was supposed to call me because of the things that had happened after running into him. Plus, I truly figured that he was faking about having what I was looking for anyway, but I kept all of that to myself as I listened to him give me directions to his house before ending the call.

"Something more important just came up." I answered to the Foot Locker employee that asked me if I needed some help as I exited the store. I was almost out of the door when a pair of gray and white Air Max caught my attention from the corner of my eye. "On second thought dirty, let me get them in a ten and a half." I paused to point at the shoe. "And please be quick about it."

Chapter Seven

"Where you get this from?" Cuzzo questioned after passing the blunt that he was smoking to Skinny.

"A nigga I know from back in the day." I answered.

We all knew B from growing up together, but he didn't want his name associated with the product. I wasn't sure why he wanted to stay behind the scenes, but it didn't bother me at all. My only real concern was the price and availability of the product, and he had come through on both of them.

"Straight up bro." Skinny paused to pass me the blunt. "This that thrax my nigga runs, what's the ticket on a zip?"

B was only charging me $3500 a pound as long as I bought more than one which roughly broke me down to $225 an ounce. The street price was somewhere in between $375 to $450 wholesale and broken down it was $20 a gram. Miser let me know that regardless of who it was or what they wanted friendship had nothing to do with business. We hustled to make money and anything that got in the way of that was bad for business. Plus I was just getting my business venture started, so I planned to take no shorts because I couldn't afford to.

"Did you hear me nigga?" Skinny questioned breaking me from my thought. "What's the ticket on a zip?"

"For you bro, give me four and a quarter." I answered before keeping the blunt moving in the rotation.

"The nigga I used to fuck wit charge $450-$500 a zip." Skinny commented.

"So what bro, what that got to do wit me?" I questioned.

"What was the key word in that sentence?" He asked Cuzzo before accepting the end of the blunt from him.

"Use my nigga. The nigga you use to fuck wit. Cause for four and a quarter he the nigga I used to fuck wit too." Cuzzo explained.

I was about to acknowledge what was being said to me, but before I could my personal line interrupted my train of thought. I hadn't heard from Moet in a couple of days, so it didn't surprise me at all to see her name on the screen of the phone.

"Hey now pretty lady, what's shaking?" I questioned after accepting her call.

"Nothing." She answered.

"What's on your mind?" I asked as I left the room with Skinny and Cuzzo.

"Where you at?" She questioned.

"I'm at the crib, why you ask that?" I responded.

"Because there's more than one person over there. As a matter of fact, who is that? And you better not say no bitch name that I don't already know about. Day I'm gonna fuck you up!" She began to rant.

I hadn't told her that I let my cousin come live with me only because I hadn't talked to her. I wasn't too sure how she would feel about it anyway, but I didn't really care. She didn't pay one bill in my residence, and the bill payers were the only ones allowed to have an opinion. She didn't share my sentiment on the subject at all, and she didn't have any problem letting it be known in terms that I could completely understand. The fact that she was Cuzzo's step-sister didn't make the situation any better, because even though they were on speaking terms, they hadn't gotten along since we were kids.

Listening to her go on and on about what kind of mistake I was making by letting him live with me did make me rethink my decision, but only while she was talking. I didn't really like him personally myself, but he was something like family. She wasn't trying to hear any part of that, and the more I tried to get her to understand where I was coming from, the more she went against it. She was adamant in her stance on the subject, and nothing that I said could move her in the other direction.

"Well let's just agree to disagree on the subject babe." I finally stated after I had heard enough.

"My momma should have never messed with his daddy, and the apple doesn't fall far from the tree. So you right Day we gonna have to agree to disagree, but don't get mad when I rub it in yo face that I told you so."

"Whatever babe." I shot back.

"I don't care if you get yo feelings hurt. I'm going out tonight, so come buy me a drink or two or three. You know where I'll be and what time I'll be there. See you then." She finished before ending our call.

"I hope you wrong babe." I thought to myself after putting my phone back in my pocket. I tried not to put too much thought into Cuzzo living with me, and her advice didn't help much either. I had other things to think about besides my living situation, and I focused on them every chance I got.

I had finally found the product that I had been looking for at the price that made it more than worth my while. My next dilemma was who I was going to sell my product to, and that was the only thing that was important to me at the time. The cocaine and heroin hustle was starting to become too dangerous for my taste, but until I got the loud thing going just as good or somewhere close, I was still stuck doing what I was doing.

"Let me get a Mike Vick bro." Skinny asked as I walked back into the front room with him and Cuzzo.

"Hundid twenty." I responded as I grabbed my digital scale, a sandwich bag, and began to weigh up the seven grams.

"Five dollars less than I'm used to paying." He paused to pull out his money and count out the hundred and twenty dollars. "I'll be one of your best customers if you keep this up."

"Whatever dirty." I responded.

"When I finished with his order, I bagged up almost two ounces and got back into traffic. I had three people waiting on me to come outside and play so they could run into me, and I wasn't about to pass up the couple of dollars that they had for me. Plus I only had Skinny Cuzzo, The Boy Wonder, and Dizal for customers for the loud and they were not enough. To make it really worth it to me I needed at least another fifty to a hundred people to spend with me, and I also knew that would never happen unless I got out in the streets and mixed and mingled with the public.

I don't have a lot of good things to say about the Department of Corrections, but when it comes to meeting drug dealers, drug users, or any other criminal for that matter, there is no other place like it. The loud hustle was just like any other drug that I sold, and the more that I bumped into old acquaintances from jail, prison, or before I went to either, the more potential customers I could pick up. As far as I was concerned, it was experiment time, and I was all for testing my theory about hustling. (The more people you know, the more money you can make.)

After accomplishing the mission that brought me out of the house in the first place, I made a quick stop at the bootleg CD shop to have a few quick words with my midnight mistress. Y wasn't really anything to look at as far as beauty was concerned because she was one of the darkest women that I have ever had the pleasure of messing with. On top of that she didn't have a fat ass or big titties to make up for what she lacked in the facial department, but what she did have was the prettiest pink pussy I had ever seen and she know how to keep what we had going on a secret, and that was important to me. She also was an avid weed smoker and that was exactly what I was in search of.

It only cost me one blunt and a few minutes of my time whispering sweet freaky shit in her ear to get her on the same page with me. She was down for almost everything that I threw her way, except the threesome that I tried to set up with her and her best friend, and that endeared her to my heart. She was also tied to the streets in a way that I couldn't pull off even if I tried. She knew about just as many people as I did because she was subject to be anywhere doing anything at any given point of the day, and that was not my style.

When I left her to get back to whatever it was that she was doing before I pulled up, I stopped at the neighborhood cell phone shop to pick up another phone. The thought had been on my mind to change my number to switch it up just in case the wrong person happened to have my number, and my new business venture gave me the excuse that I needed to do so. I planned to turn my hustle all the way over to loud and loud only, so I ended up getting another phone that I planned to dedicate strictly to that. I also ended up picking up the owner of the shop as a new customer, and that worked out perfectly for me.

--

From there I caught a couple of sells before stopping at Latoya's house to pay her a visit. I hadn't spent any time with her since she brought Eri by my house to give me a sexual workout that I will probably always remember. I felt kind of bad for some odd reason about that, and it all became clear to me why when she cussed me out for neglecting her. I didn't really feel like I was, but after getting her side of the story and processing the information, I completely understood where she was coming from. It didn't move me in the slightest either way but I did apologize for my actions because I knew that was all she really wanted.

Layla decided that she wanted to talk to me as soon as I got back in my car, and that was a blessing in and of itself. She still hadn't put forth any effort to make it up to me for our lunch date incident, but I keep my thoughts about it to myself I wasn't really in a rush to do anything to her because my experience had taken the attention to another step that I needed to make before I headed home, so after I came back to our conversation, I caught just the end of what she was saying to me.

She must have known that my mind was on something else, because before I could get the question out of my mouth, she repeated the most important part of what she had said to me.

She would be off of work for a week in three days, and she hadn't forgot about making it up to me, so I would have to free myself up and make some real time for her. I didn't have a problem with that all, so after agreeing on a time, place and date for the hook up, I ended our call and got right back in traffic.

"Damn I need a clone." I thought to myself as I detoured to bump into another one of my good geeks. The last heroin package that I had comped was a little over an ounce, and if everything went anywhere close to how I had planned it would, that would be the last package I needed. I had enough money put up to hold me down for the next six months if the need arose but that was not good enough. I refuse to cold turnkey what had been taking care of me until I was truly certain that I had something else that would at least come close to being a substitute. Plus I had enough pill customers to ensure that I seen close to if not more than a couple thousand dollars a day, and that was hard to let go of.

By the time I made my last stop and got home the sun had set and the night was upon me. I had been a lot of places, and seen a lot of things, but there was no place like my city. During the day law and order ruled without too much interference, but when the sun set things changed. The night changed. The night belonged to the streets and the rules of engagement were not in the favor of the police. So much so, that even stopping at a red light or stop sign was situational and in most cases a bad idea.

After changing my clothes and putting together a club package that contained fifty-six ½ gram bags, I sat around and listed to Cuzzo, Skinny and The Boy Wonder swap stories about their hustling exploits. My day had been extremely dull in comparison, so I just nodded my head and kept my thoughts to myself Since Cuzzo came to live with me it seemed like he had brought The Boy Wonder and Skinny with him, but it didn't surprise me at all. They were always together or not too far apart no matter where he was, so I really didn't expect anything different in our situation.

When I had finally heard enough, I grabbed the package, the gun, my keys, and made my way towards the door. I was almost out of the house when Skinny stopped me for a fifty bag. The Boy Wonder bought something for thirty, and Cuzzo wanted something for twenty.

"A quick dollar and I ain't even left the house." I thought to myself as I walked to my car. Checking my surrounding before pulling off was a habit that I had picked up from my uncle, and I was glad for it because I hesitated just long enough for the police to ride down the street before pulling off. "This should be an interesting night." I said as I pulled out of my driveway and went in the opposite direction as the police went.

It only took me a few minutes to get downtown from my house because the speed limit was meaningless to me. The rule was to get from point A to Point B as fast as possible, and I followed it to the letter. My only problem was finding somewhere close to the club to park just in case I needed to make a faster get away. That took me longer to do than I did to get there, and it bothered me to no end.

I was almost ready to give up and go home, but on my third lap around the area, a parking space mysteriously appeared right on the side of the club. It was so close in fact that I passed it up and had to back up to pull into it. I'm not all that good at parallel parking, but I pulled it off to almost perfection on the first try.

"Day what took you so long to get here?" Moet questioned as she gave me a hug. "And please tell me that ain't no gun and you just extremely happy to see me.

"First I couldn't find anywhere I wanted to park, and yes I am extremely happy to see you, but that is my gun." I whispered in her ear.

"As long as you extremely happy to see me I don't care about the gun. Buy me a drink and promise me you not gonna start shooting in here." She stated before breaking our embrace.

"I got you covered on the first one, but I can't make any promises on the last one." I responded.

"For the next couple of hours we got chocolate wasted off of shots of 1738 Remy Martin with no chaser and partied like rock stars. My club package almost disappeared as fast as I broke it out, and that truly took me by surprise. Moet knew almost everybody in the club, and as soon as she put the word out I was in business; ten here, twenty there, thirty there. It was amazing how fast it moved.

Just to make sure that I kept my experiment going I made sure that I put that money in a different pocket to keep track of it; ten here, twenty there, twenty there.

"This shit might just work out like I want it to." I thought to myself as a downed my fifth, sixth, or seventh shot. I wasn't sure exactly how much that I had to drink, but I did know that I was fast approaching my limit. Moet must have been thinking the same though, because before I could get my thoughts and mouth on the same page, she pulled me into her arms.

"You going home with me, and I ain't taking no for an answer." She whispered in my ear.

Chapter Eight

"That's them people." I said to myself as I looked at the all tinted up black Grand Prix. I had seen it on more than one occasion while I was out and about hustling, but at no point in time had I ever seen who was actually inside of the car. It looked exactly like something that a hustler would be riding in, and those where the exact type of cars that the St. Louis Drug Task Force (aka the Jump Out Boys) liked to drive. It made it easier for them to pull up and jump out on any given drug set because it fit right in, and it also gave them a better chance in the high speed car chases that went with the life because they handled better that the marked black and white ones did.

"If it is, they don't want this." I laughed to myself as I took one last look, then turned into traffic. Moet had hooked me up with a brand new SRT Jeep Cherokee, and it was one of the fastest vehicles that I had ever had the pleasure to drive. It made getting from point A to point B an experience no matter where I happened to be going. It was actually like it was made to be driven fast, and that was right up my alley.

After checking my mirrors and noticing that the GP had pulled out and was trailing me, my personal line decided to ring.

"Hey now Layla babe, what's shaking momma?" I questioned after answering the phone.

"Did you get my text sir?" She questioned.

"No ma'am, please remind me." I answered as I checked my rear view mirror to see if I still had company.

"The one about our reservations at Ruth Chris at 8pm." She reminded me.

The thought crossed my mind to inform her that I didn't need to be reminded, but before I could open my mouth and let the words slide out, the truck lit up with red, white, and blue lights.

"It's a quarter 'til babe, I'm like fifteen minutes away." I explained.

"Don't be late." She warned me.

"Not a problem. One." I shot back before ending our call and putting the phone in my pocket.

I had been involved in countless police chases since I started hustling, so the flashing lights didn't bother me at all. Being that I was in the middle of the intersection workout put perfect for what I had planned, so I turned on my blinker to signal that I wanted to get over.

As I checked my surroundings I noticed another unmarked car coming up on my left to assist with my stop, and that was not a part of my plan. I had planned to let the GP stop then take off after they got out, but since that no longer seemed logical with help coming for them, as soon as I got over I put my foot on the gas pedal before the other car had the chance to be of any help to the one behind me.

Turning up the music as I made a quick right on Goodfellow from West Florissant, I made another quick right on the side street North Point. Unconcerned with the traffic laws or the police, I ran both stop signs then made a left on Park Lane.

Checking the rear view mirror as I made a quick right on Gladys. I didn't see the flashing lights anymore so I took it to Riverview and made a left.

As soon as I hit Swtizer, I saw a marked car out of the corner of my eye so I made a right on McLaren and took it to Halls Ferry. At Halls Ferry I made another right and took it to Broadway.

The thought crossed my mind to stay on Broadway and take it all the way downtown, but it didn't last long, so as soon as I got to Calvery I made a right and took it back to West Florissant. Made a right on West Florissant then a left on Union. Ran both stop signs, all three lights, then made a left on Bircher and veered left as I got on the highway.

As I blew exit after exit going no less than one hundred and ten miles an hour, I lost sight of the several sets of lights that had joined the chase, but I didn't care. My main concern was to out run their radios, and as I exited at the downtown exit I wasn't sure that I had, but I wasn't sure that I hadn't either.

I knew that I would find out sooner or later, so I pushed the thought from my mind and continued to my destination. Ruth Chris sat inside of the Hyatt where Layla worked and that was a blessing that I didn't even have to pray for.

"Cuzzo you might be good for something after all." I said to myself as I jumped out of the jeep and tossed the keys to the valet. He had told me how he had used the same move on a high speed chase that he had gotten himself into, and I had never forgotten about it.

After getting my ticket, I walked into the Hyatt with my goodie bag that contained the gun, drugs, and all of the paraphernalia that made my life work, and made a b-line straight to the restaurant. Checking the clock on the wall it truly surprised me that I was a few minutes early.

"Walk-in or reservation?" Questioned the hostess.

"Reservation." I answered before giving her Layla's last name.

"This way sir." She stated as she led me inside of the restaurant.

"Right on time I see." Layla commented as I sat down at the table with her.

"I try my best." I responded.

"What you do today? She questioned.

"You want the truth, or do you want me to lie to you?" I answered.

"Truth always." She said as she rolled her eyes then took a sip of her drink.

The thought crossed my mind to down play my day to make it seem as uneventful as possible because I wasn't sure how she would respond to the truth, but that wasn't what she wanted to hear, so I took a few minutes to give her a quick rundown of what I had done all the way up to me sitting down at the table across from her.

When I finished my story there was a strange moment of silence between us, and for some odd reason it didn't feel right to me. I wasn't sure that I should have been completely honest about my activities, but before I could think of something to fill in the empty space her facial expression changed and she started laughing.

"Well that worked out perfect for me." She paused to get her laughter under control. "Because now I know that I have you all to myself."

"Indeed you do pretty lady cause I ain't fucking with that car until at least shift change for the Jump Out Boys." I explained.

"Good. I'm glad you valeted because I have a suite lined up after we eat, so hopefully you don't have any plans for the rest of the evening and most of the morning until check out time." She said.

The thought crossed my mind to question her about what else she had planned for me, but before I could get it out our waiter made his appearance. I had looked over the menu briefly while we talked, but I still hadn't made up my mind on what I wanted, so I ordered a drink for myself and let him know that we still needed a few minutes more to get out orders together.

My grandfather had told me on more than one occasion that when a man and a woman are at a restaurant that it is the man's job to place the order for both her and himself, and I never forgot that advice, so after our waiter left I took a second to see what she wanted while I made up my mind. When he brought back my drink I placed our orders and I could see from the look on her face that she was impressed by how I handled the situation.

Since three questions got us to this point in our lives, I felt like it would be the perfect way to converse while we enjoyed our meal, so after we were back alone I brought the idea to her attention and she agreed with a simple nod of her head and a raise of her drink.

"How does this night end if you have it the way you want it to?" I questioned.

My question must have caught her completely off guard, because instead of the quick response that I had gotten used to dealing with from her, she just stared at me. I figured that she was trying to get her answer together so I just enjoyed my Patron margarita and the silence that came with it.

"If this night ends the way I want it to, I will be sleeping comfortably when I get the call to check out." She answered.

"And what makes you sleep comfortably?" I shot back.

"Orgasms." She responded.

"And what makes you orgasm?" I asked more interested than I had ever been in one of her answers.

"Now that's the best question you have ever asked me." She paused to take a sip of her drink. "But before I answer that I have to ask you a question."

"It counts against your three, but knock yourself out." I responded.

"Do you eat pussy?" She inquired.

"Of course." I answered.

"Well with that said, you can make me orgasm by first eating my pussy." She paused as the waiter returned and placed our food on the table. "And when you got me all the way in the mood with that then you gonna have to finish me off with every position that you can think of. And please be inventive."

The thought crossed my mind to ask her about how many positions she actually knew, but my food looked and smelled too good to ignore even for our conversation. She must have felt the same way, because before I could say grace and get started, she was already eating. I couldn't argue with her on that issue even if I wanted to, so I thanked God for the day and followed her lead and dug in.

The steak was cooked perfectly and tasted like perfection; the potato came with butter and sour cream, needing just a little salt and pepper to season it up. My run in with the law had done nothing to ruin my appetite, so I went to work without a second thought about it. My phone decided to sing to me when I was cutting up my steak into small pieces like I like it.

"Can you turn off you phones/ ringers until me and you part ways? And yes I know that is my second question." She stated with just a hint of attitude in her voice.

"Not a problem babe." I responded because I knew that my day of hustling had ended as soon as I refused to stop for the police.

Under any other circumstance I probably would have laughed, refused, or just go up and walked out, but that was not the case. Plus as far as I was concerned seeing Layla orgasm was the most important thing to me at that moment, and I refused to do or let anything interfere with that. Sampling her pleasures was an experience that I had yet to enjoy, while getting money was an old friend, and I have always been a sucker for new things.

The rest our meal went by with a couple more drinks and general conversation, and it truly surprised me that though we talked about several different subjects, Layla didn't word anything that she said into a question form. When the check was finally brought she refused to let me pay the bill because our dinner was her idea and she had it covered. Against her wishes I added a few more dollars to the tip just to feel like I made some form of a contribution to the meal.

I wasn't sure how she truly felt about it because she just stared at me from across the table as she finished her drink. The thought crossed my mind to inquire about it, but since I had already used my three questions, I kept it to myself and finished my own drink as I returned her stare.

"Do you think you can handle me?" She questioned as she slid the room key across the table."If so, I will be in the Presidential suite waiting to see what you got for me." She ended as she got up and walked away from the table.

Chapter Nine

"Hey now Moet, what's shaking babe?" I questioned after accepting her call.

"Where you at?" She asked.

"I'm in traffic." I answered.

"Where you going?" She shot back.

"To the house to change clothes." I responded.

After parting ways with Layla and turning my phones back up I found out how many calls I had missed and who they were from. The text messages were more than I cared to count, so instead of going through them to see exactly what I had missed, I just cleared them all out. Moet's name and number was one that I did remember seeing as I scrolled through, but I deleted it along with the rest of them.

The thought crossed my mind to explain to her why I hadn't answered my phone or responded to her text messages before she got around to asking me about it, but I kept my thought to myself. Explaining my actions to her would not stop her from wanting to know all of the dirty details of my evening with Layla when she found out that was the reason I turned my ringers off, so I just held the phone and waited patiently for the game of twenty questions that I knew was about to begin.

"Day you already know where this conversation is about to go so please don't make me have to ask you a thousand and one questions to get the whole story out of you." Moet stated.

Moet knew just as well as I did that I would not pull over for the police when I was out hustling, so that part of the story about me taking off on them and high speeding though the streets didn't move her at all. She was a tad bit amused by the valet parking move to hide my car, but when she found out that it was Layla that I was going to meet up with, the sound of her voice changed a couple of octaves.

"So you took her to Ruth Chris, Day? You ain't NEVER took me to Ruth Chris!" She said with a true hint of jealousy in her tone.

"Do you want to know what happened or do you want to talk about what I ain't did with you?" I questioned.

Due to the fact that I really paid for our first lunch date no mind, I had forgotten to bring Moet up to speed on what had happened. From her breathing and grunting I could tell that she was not happy at all about being left out of the loop, but there was nothing that I could do about it. I wasn't sure exactly how she felt about it, and I really don't care. There was no changing what had already been done, and moving forward was my only concern because yesterday was over with and tomorrow was too far away to think about All I had was the day in front of me and that was all that I was looking forward to.

   Though I already had it in my mind that I would fuck the shit out of Layla when the opportunity presented itself to me, I was truly surprised by what transpired. I had all intentions of kissing and licking her from the top of her head to the bottom of her feet, then putting her down for the count after, and even though it worked out according to plan in the end, getting the desired result took much more effort than I actually though it would.

   Moet couldn't contain her amusement as I recapped the erotic trials and tribulations that I had to endure dealing with Layla, but it didn't bother me at all. Layla seemed to take our sexual competition just as personal as I took it, and given a different time, place, or situation, she might have gotten the better of me instead of almost getting the better of me. Moet knew exactly what I meant, and still gave Layla credit for almost coming close, but my uncle always told me that almost only counts with horseshoes and hand grenades, and that's what I told her in response.

The thought crossed my mind to tell her exactly what happened when I finally put Layla down, but I kept that to myself. It was a first for me, and until I experienced it again, I planned to hold that little piece of information close to my chest.

My business line must have known that I didn't have anything else important to share with Moet because it started to sing to me just as I started to wrap up our call. She completely understood my business before pleasure modus operandi, and let me go after making me promise that I would meet up with her after she go off of work. I was almost home at that point in our call, but I detoured to meet up with my caller. The money wasn't all that important to me, but it was just enough that I wasn't going to pass it up either.

By the time I actually made it home, it was well into the wonderful afternoon hustling hours, and my phone showed it. My intentions were to change clothes, smoke a blunt, and play Call of Duty on my X-Box 360 for a few minutes, but that was not to be the case. Duty called in the form of several deliveries that I needed to make, and several other stops that needed to be made, and following the dollar took precedence over the simple pleasures. So much so, that I only stayed in the house long enough to restock my goodie bag, sell Cuzzo and Skinny fifty bags, and send out a mass media text to all of my customers to let them know that I was coming outside to play, then I was right back in traffic.

Not to be outdone by my business line, my personal line decided that it wanted to match it call for call. And though it didn't bother or surprise me at all, it did keep me extremely busy for the rest of the afternoon.

When things finally slowed down, I made my way back home to get myself together. I had showered before parting ways with Layla, but due to the fact that I put the same clothes right back on, I decided that I needed to shower again. Plus for some odd reason running the streets leaves a certain type of odor on the body, and though it doesn't stink, Moet let it be known early in our relationship that she didn't like it at all.

I wasn't sure exactly what she might want to do when we got together, so after showering, smoking, and playing the game like I had planned earlier and not gotten around to, I found myself standing inside of my walk-in closet just staring at my clothes. I wasn't sure if it was the large variety of items that I had to choose from, or the fact that the last package that I had bought from B was arguably the best weed that I had ever had the pleasure to inhale. Either way I couldn't make up my mind on what I wanted to put on, and as I smoked a cigarette to boost my high past where it really needed to be, I stood lost in thought about what my next move should be.

The hustle came with so many different benefits, and the clothes, shoes, accessories, and cars were the status symbols to show just how good your hustle happened to be. Back in the day when I first started out if you spent a hundred dollars on some jeans, fifty dollars for a shirt, and maybe a hunded fitty for some shoes you were doing better that average, but that was then. As I looked through my wardrobe still undecided on what I wanted to wear, it dawned on me that I had shoes the cost almost a thousand dollars a pair, belts that cost half that, and jeans that cost half of that.

"This shit crazy." I said to myself as I grabbed an outfit and did the math on exactly how much I had paid for it.

I don't know how long exactly it took me to finally get dressed, but when I was finished the missed calls and texts reminded me of the other things that I could be doing besides worrying about the money that I had already spent. My uncle's favorite line about the price of an item popped into my head and I couldn't do anything but smile about it, because his wisdom spoke volumes towards the hustle and anything and everything connected to it. (If you worry about what it cost, then you probably can't afford it.)

Browsing through my call logs I saw nothing that really moved me at all until I got to a text from Layla. I hadn't heard from her since we parted ways in the lobby of the hotel, and for some odd reason that didn't sit right with me. I couldn't put my finger on the why of the situation, but I felt some type of way about it.

My mother used to always preach to me about women and the games they would play with men. Her colorful sayings and words of wisdom always had a delayed effect on one side of the coin, but on the flip side of it, they were always right on time. (Don't worry about what a woman says when she speaks, worry about what she means, because more often than not they are two different things.)

So instead of just taking the "Thanx, slept beautifully" text at face value, I put a little thought into what she actually meant before I responded. Being under the influence didn't help my situation either. As a matter of fact, it heightened by thought process to another level and made me over think her meaning. On top of that I had a few other things running through my mind at the same time, and those had to be taken into account also.

"What you doing tonight?" Cuzzo questioned from the top of the steps breaking me from my thoughts and bringing me back to the moment.

"I'm gonna step out and bump into this lil bitch for a drink or what not, why what's shaking?" I answered as I finally decided on what I wanted to say to Layla.

"Cause we gonna step out too, and you know where we gonna end up, so come fuck with us if you get the chance to." He explained.

The thought crossed my mind to decline the offer, but the hustler inside of me knew that there would probably be a couple of dollars in it for me if I did, and that motivated my decision more than anything else.

"I'll see." I responded as I typed in my three question response to Layla's text.

After spraying myself with some Sean John cologne and getting my hustler kit together, I left the house and got into traffic. Moet had texted me earlier with the time and place she wanted me to get face to face with her and I kept that in the forefront of my mind as I bent a couple of corners and made a few deliveries.

She had a thing about being fashionably late to anything that she did, and that worked out to my advantage. So much so, that I had the chance to make several more stops, bump into a few more of my customers, and make a quick appearance at the dice game.

"I'm gone right after I catch the dice." I said to myself. I had lost a couple thousand dollars the last time that I found myself in the crap house, but that was just a part of the game. It was either win some or lose some in those situations, because breaking even was a waste of time for me.

By the time the dice made it around the circle to me, I had already started building up my bank from the numerous side bets and fades that I had taken while I waited. I wasn't sure about how my luck would be, but since I was already playing with somebody else's money, I threw the extras around with reckless abandon.

"It's time to start cuffing." I said to myself after I hit my fifth point in a row. Tens and fours, nines and sixes, sixes and eights, and at least two straight bets to go along with the fade. It didn't make a difference what point that I caught because not only did I make it, but I also had another bet going on to go with it. The money was coming in so fast that I had stopped keeping track of it as I stuffed bills in my other three pockets. The thought crossed my mind that I couldn't miss, so I tested the theory and gave away and be that came my way. Bars, comes, craps, or naturals, anything over or under a six, and my personal favorite, the make or miss in three rolls.

   I can't say how long I had the dice but by the time I let go of them I had cleaned our several of the players and the bets were coming and going in every direction. My uncle taught me the game when I was little and his number one rule was "never stick around long enough to lose back what you won". It made sense to me in more ways than one, but I rarely abided by it. I had my own rule that I lived and died by and my all or nothing strategy had either worked out or failed horribly on more occasions than I cared to count.

The thought of walking away was the last thing on my mind until my personal phone broke my train of thought about the money in front of me with an incoming call from Layla. Not to be outdone at that moment my business line began to sing a half a second later with an incoming call from one of my good geeks, and it put me in an awkward situation. I was torn between which one to answer first and I hesitated for a split second then grabbed the one that was more important to me. "Hey now, where you at?"

After getting the money all situated, I answered Layla's call and received a verbal response to the three questions that I had texted her before I left my house. Yes, her text had more than one meaning to it. Yes, she wanted to do it with me again. And most importantly to me, yes her orgasms are always a sight to behold. I figured that the answers to my questions would all be yeses, but I asked anyway just because I wanted to be certain of my thought. Assuming that I knew the answer to my own questions with a woman had gotten me in trouble on more than one occasion, and there was something about her that made me not want to have any misunderstandings that could be avoided.

Lost in my conversation with Layla the dice made it back to me and passed me by, and it didn't bother me at all. I was actually looking for a good enough reason to leave anyway, and as soon as I ended our call, my business line sung me my way out.

"I truly appreciate everybody's contributions to my night on the town, so until next time have a nice night fellows." I stated before bowing and making my exit from the gambling house to my car. My customer was already parked behind my car, so after taking care of her order, I jumped in the jeep, started it up, checked my surrounding, got myself together, fired up the half a blunt I had left in the ashtray, then got into traffic.

By the time I made in to the corner, my personal line rung again and I knew exactly who it was before I looked at the screen.

"Where the fuck you at Day?" Moet screamed in my ear. "And you better not be with no bitch.

Chapter Ten

My uncle told me when I finally decided to jump off of the porch and start playing the streets that "the two hardest things to juggle will be the money and the women that come with it". I had heard what he said every time that he preached it to me, but I wasn't really listening like I should have been. His words of wisdom were always taken with a grain of salt for me, but when they became clear, they always hit me like a ton of bricks and made more sense than they should have.

I had always kept a couple of dollars coming in along with a few women to enjoy them with. My loud experiment going much better than I ever thought It would, my consumption of both dead presidents and women that came along with them had reached a level that was almost exhausting to keep up with.

I'm tired as a motherfucker." I said to myself as I crawled out of the bed to pick my pants up off the floor to get my phones out of the pockets.

"Day come back to bed." Layla ordered.

The thought crossed my mind to do exactly what she said, but it only lasted for a split second I had not even planned to end up sleeping at her apartment because I had something else up my sleeve for my night, but she called right on time and said just what I wanted to hear. Plus since I had opened my door to my cousin, I rarely slept in my own bed. Layla used that little piece of information to her advantage, and it didn't bother me at all.

"So are you coming back to bed on your own, or do I have to persuade you?" She questioned breaking me from my thought.

"I definitely prefer persuasion if I have a choice in the matter." I responded as I scrolled through both call and text logs to see what all I had missed while I was asleep.

"By force it is baby." She paused just long enough to get out of the bed. "Are you sure that you don't want to reconsider?"

The thought crossed my mind to respond, but before I could she had squatted down in front of me and put my dick in her mouth. It wasn't hard yet, but it only took a few strokes and a couple of licks to get my juices flowing in that direction. I was still reading through my text messages as she caught her rhythm, and the erotic pictures that were attached to a message that came from a woman that I had met a couple of days before helped to further arouse me.

Her fellatio technique was not the best that I had ever had, but it definitely wasn't the worst either. It was somewhere in between good and great, and as her mouth lubricated and her hands stroked; my phones were starting to become an irrelevant thing to me. I had seen that nothing really important was in need of my immediate attention besides a few dollars that was waiting on me to pick it up, and I was really in no rush to do that.

"You win babe." I paused just long enough to throw my phones on the bed. "I'm getting back in the bed."

By the time I finally left her apartment it was well into the afternoon rush. My business line would not stop singing no matter how many times I answered it, and that told me that my loud experiment was turning out better than I thought it would. Layla did not share my sentiment on the subject, but I paid her no mind. What I considered to be the sound of money, she considered them to be interruptions to our quality time together, so we eventually agreed to disagree on this issue, leaving both of our opinions on the subject intact.

Ten stops later I was around the corner from my house and something caught my attention. I wasn't actually sure what it was, but it stopped me in my tracks. My uncle used to always tell me to follow my first mind when it came to funny feelings and intuitions, and I had paid very close attention to that piece of advice. It had kept me out of trouble and the line of fire on more occasions than I can think of. But on the flip side of the coin, every time that I transgressed that advice it never worked out to my advantage. Not following my instincts had gotten me shot, jumped on, locked up, and almost killed, not to mention all of the arguments and disagreements that I had gotten myself into when they could have been avoided.

Turning on my street I caught sight of a white van turning the corner at the other end of the block. I almost didn't pay it any attention but I changed my mind and decided to see where my funny feeling would lead me.

Putting my foot on the gas pedal just a little more, I made the two left turns and caught sight of the van within seconds. It was just making a right turn onto Jennings Station Rd.

I didn't want to catch all the way up to the van, so instead I let a car get in front of me before I made the turn myself. I wasn't sure why I was following the van or what I expected to find out for my trouble, but once I got into traffic I was determined to see it through.

"This shit crazy." I thought to myself as I fired up the half of a blunt that was in my ashtray.

Keeping my distance while keeping my line of sight directed on my target, when the van turned to get on the highway, my funny feeling came right back to me in full force. My business line started to sing as I made the turn myself, but I paid it no mind. Something about the plain white panel van in front of me had truly grabbed the whole of my attention, and I couldn't shake it.

The speed limit on the highway was not a law that I followed in normal situations since I started driving, and it really went out of the window when I started hustling, so as I smoked and stayed at 55 mph I felt like I was doing something wrong. My business line sung again as I switched lanes and I notice that it was Cuzzo calling.

The thought crossed my mind to ignore his call like I had the one before it, but I went against my first mind and grabbed the phone.

"Hey now."

"Where you at in the world?" He questioned.

"On the highway" I answered.

"Coming or going?" He shot back.

"Going. I'm headed towards downtown. What's shaking?" I questioned.

"What you got going on?" He asked.

The thought crossed my mind to lie or something extremely close to it, but I went against that thought also and ran down the series of event that led to where I was and where I was going. I wasn't sure exactly what he would have to say about it, or what he would think about my wild goose chase, but it didn't surprise me at all that he was all for it. He was probably the most paranoid person that I knew other than myself when it came to the police, and it didn't hurt that he had been a fugitive from the law for years.

This only made him more curious about what the outcome of my trip would be, and that only made me think more about it myself. So much so, that I had to get off of the phone with him because he started asking too many questions that I didn't have the answers to.

When the van got off at the downtown exit I was right behind it, and at the end of my blunt. Several things ran through my mind at that time, but none of them really made any real sense to me. I couldn't see who exactly was in the van nor could I tell what kind of van it was because it didn't have any identifying markings or advertisements on the sides. All I knew for sure was that at that moment I was playing follow the leader and my fingertips were getting hot.

As I passed all of the shops, stores, and buildings in my pursuit the weed had me feeling carefree and in the mood to shop. At Tucker I made the left, then at Market I made another left, then at Market I made another left, then my heart stopped beating.

"Oh Shit!" I screamed at myself as the van turned into the Federal Building parking lot. The sight alone removed any feeling that the weed had given me instantaneously, and my emotional state quickly ran the gamut from paranoid to extremely afraid.

The thought crossed my mind to head straight back to my house, but I pushed that thought from my mind. Home for me for some odd reason didn't seem like a safe place to be at that moment. I had heard that home was where the heart was at, but after coming to grips with the sight of that van turning into the Federal Building, I was certain that my heart was no longer a part of my body. I still wasn't sure about exactly what I had seen and what it actually meant towards my life at that moment or the future, but I was absolutely positive that it would not be good in the end.

My personal line rung and broke me from my train of negative what if thoughts and brought me back to reality. It surprised me that the call was from Diosa, but at that point in my life I paid it no mind as I grabbed the phone.

"Hey now babe. What's shaking?" I answered.

"Where you at Day?" She questioned.

"I'm actually right around the corner from your house." I responded.

"Pull up then." She requested.

"Here I come." I answered before ending the call and tossing the phone back on the passenger's seat next to my business line.

I had told Cuzzo that I would call him back when I got to the bottom of my follow the leader thing I had gotten started, but I couldn't bring myself to do it. I actually refused to answer my business line again until I changed the number, so I reached over and turned it off, the tossed it back on the seat.

When I pulled into the parking lot of the apartment building that Diosa lived in, she was standing outside waiting on me. After everything else that had happened since I had gotten out of the bed. I didn't know how to take that. I wasn't sure if it was a good thing or a bad one, but I was almost positive that it was a first

"What's the biz babe?" I questioned after the hug and kiss that we always shared as our greeting.

"Day I miss you." She paused to give me her sad face. "Like I really miss you."

Only one thing crossed my mind after her statement, and it had nothing to do with her missing me. Diosa was a lot of things to the world, but the missing a man type was not one of them. She had been a part of my life long enough for me to know almost everything that I really needed to know about her, and her words were then second most important thing to me on that list. Her G-spot was the first one, but it only mattered when I missed her, and that was not the case at that time.

"What's wrong babe? As a matter of fact, fuck what's wrong, what can I do to make it better babe?" I questioned.

Instead of responding to my question she grabbed my hand and led me inside of her building. I had all kinds of things running through my mind, and the distraction of just being in her presence was welcomed regardless of how much it was probably going to cost me in the end.

By the time we exited the elevator and made it to her fifth floor loft, I was truly in the mood for whatever she had up her sleeve for me. The gentle sway of her hips from side to side was hypnotizing, and the Bath and Body Works aroma that she was giving off just added to it. For a split second having my way with her was the only thought on my mind, and I was not bothered by it at all.

    Once we got inside of her apartment reality kicked back in an my mind started running through every possible scenario that I could come up with on the pros and cons of the situation that was at hand. If my eyes were not playing tricks on me, which I knew that they were not, nothing that I could come up with had a good outcome for me to go with it. No matter what kind of spin I put on it, it kept coming back to the same two facts. I was not only a convicted felon from my past run-ins with the law, I was also still on parole for those transgressions.

    Diosa could tell that my thoughts were preoccupied by something other than her, and she played her role to perfection. Holding me close to her and not saying a word was exactly what I needed as I worked through the thousand and one possibilities that all ended with me taking another extended vacation from the streets, and that was all I could ask for. The fact that her cuddling came with a lot of rubbing and touching only added to the beauty of the situation, and it was a plus.

"It's gonna be what it's gonna be." I finally said to myself. There were so many ifs that went along with my situation, but I refused to sell myself a dream when I knew that I couldn't afford it. The life that I lived came with consequences, and I had already accepted them for what they were before I started back hustling. There was no reason to worry about what I couldn't change. I had heard the Serenity Prayer while on vacation, and it stuck the first time. "God grant me the serenity to accept the things that I cannot change, the courage to change the things that I can, and the wisdom to know the difference."

After a few more minutes of silence, I go myself back together and moved on.

"You alright now Day?" She questioned.

"Yeah I'm straight now babe." I paused as I returned some of her rubs." What's up with you?"

Her answer was truly and completely one that I was not expecting or prepared for, but I took it on the chin. The start and middle of my day had already been an exercise in the unpredictability of life, so it kind of made sense in some strange type of way. I wasn't really all that interested in living with her and being in a committed relationship with her, because I had all kinds of things going on in my world, but for a split second I did think about it. As a matter of fact, I had actually thought about it seriously for a few minutes after my split second of thinking about it, and I still came up with the same answer. In my mind, I would need a little more than an invitation from a beautiful woman to make me give up the freedom that having my own everything afforded me, and Diosa's argument was not strong enough to change my mind on the subject.

The conversation lasted much longer than I thought it would, and I found myself explaining myself more than I thought I should have to. I don't know if it was all for her benefit or if something inside of me needed to hear my own reasons for turning down the opportunity to wake up with her every morning. But whatever it was, I just couldn't bring myself to agree to the arrangement. The con of having to end up in the same bed every night far outweighed the pro of being able to sleep where and with whom I pleased, and that fact stuck with me to the point that I couldn't shake it loose.

After hugs, kisses, and the promise that would be front and center at the club to donate to her cause, I left Diosa's loft and got back in traffic. The incident from earlier in the day was still in the forefront of my mind in a major way, and I had yet to take some form of proper precautions so my next stop was to This, That, and the Other. My neighborhood telephone guy had a shop inside of the resale shop owned by one of my old friends Snacc Man.

I had been planning on changing my phones and numbers, and the situation at hand worked out perfectly for the switch. I wasn't sure if my thoughts about the Feds watching me, my cousin, my house, or anybody connected to me were even legitimate, but I usually followed my fist mind and this situation would get treated the same way. It didn't matter to me if my phones had bugs or taps on them, because the statement "better safe than sorry was truth in the simplest form. Yuri charged me cash for the phones I wanted, but took loud as payment for the service, and that worked out perfectly for me. After leaving the shop, I bent a couple of corners before I pulled up to my house. My cousin, Skinny and the Boy Wonder were sitting around talking about everything and nothing, and it didn't surprise me at all. I hadn't talked to Cuzzo since I ended our previous conversation, and he was extremely interested in getting every piece of information from me that he could on that issue.

I didn't really have anything new to add to the information that he already knew from our first talk, but Skinny had his own pieces to the puzzle that he wanted to add, and it threw me for a loop. His mother didn't hustle at all, or for that matter from the only and only time that I had met her, she didn't even condone our lifestyles, but she had informed him that somebody was following her around the city and she didn't have the slightest idea of who it was. She had her own ideas, but she wasn't certain about any of them.

"This can't be good." I thought to myself as Skinny finished adding his two cents. Cuzzo wanted more information on the issue before he made up his mind on the subject, but I did not share his sentiment. I wasn't sure what I wanted to do about it, but I was positive that something had to be done.

After changing clothes and sending out a mass media text about the changing of my number, Layla was the first person to call me back to let me know that she had received my message. It surprised me just a little bit, but I pushed it from my mind. I had so much other stuff to think about that I just smiled to myself and kept it pushing. My business line started singing, and I focused on that while I tried to make up my mind if I wanted to give my new number to Cuzzo, Skinny, or the Boy Wonder, I had just recently paid the bill on the number that they had for me, so I finally decided to just keep that phone around just in case one of them called, then I got back into business.

Chapter Eleven

"Day let me ask you something." Layla proposed as we stood in front of my house talking.

"Come on with it." I responded.

"If I asked you to move in with me, what would you say?" She inquired.

The thought crossed my mind to say no without giving what she said any thought, but I bit my tongue. It had been almost a week since Diosa asked me the exact same question, so I took it as a sign.

"If you asked me to move in with you, I would say give me a reason that I can't argue with or refute." I answered.

"Just one reason?" She shot back.

"Yep." I responded.

"Ok." She paused as she moved in close until we were face-to-face."There are well over a hundred thousand dollars worth of cars parked in front of this house, and not one of you niggas has a job."

I hadn't really paid too much attention to the Jeep Cherokee that I drove, the Dodge Charger Cuzzo drove, the Chrysler 300 Skinny drove, or the Chrysler 300 SRT that The Boy Wonder drove.

I asked Layla to give me one reason and her response was not anywhere close to what I thought that she might say. As a matter of fact, as I took a quick inventory of all of our cars, I couldn't think of any response that would refute what she had said. I was actually at a loss for words for a split second as I thought about the drive that I made downtown following that van, but after I got my words back working, I told her to follow me in the house.

My first thought was to come up with something that sounded extremely clever as a rebuttal to her statement, but when we made it to my room I kept my thoughts to myself as I started to inventory my belongings. I didn't need anything in the furniture department because she had a very nice thing going on in her apartment so after I got my thoughts on the matter all the way together, I headed straight for my walk-in closet and started grabbing clothes and shoes and stacking them up.

It surprised me for a split second when she grabbed the box of trash bags from the shelf and began to load them up one after the other with my things.

"This lady here might be a keeper." I said to myself after she left with a bag to take to her car.

When she came back to grab another bag, I couldn't do anything but smile at her. I had planned to do everything myself, but she wouldn't listen to me on the subject. Her response was something close to the "teamwork makes the dream work" speech, and it truly amused me to no end. My laugh brought one from her and that broke the silence that we had been working in. When that moment passed I returned to the closet to finish pulling out my wardrobe, and she went right back to packing and loading.

I can't say how many trips that I made in and out of my walk-in closet, but it took her seven trips to get all of the bags in her car. The last two were filled with shoes, and she really earned my respect because she handled them as if they weighed next to nothing when I knew that wasn't the case at all.

"I got a little rearranging to do." She explained after she came back from the last trip to the car. So I'm out of here and I'll see you at home later." She finished before giving me a kiss and leaving.

Since I had my own personal door to come and go as I pleased, when I went back upstairs no one in the house had any idea that I had sent most of my clothes with Layla. I wasn't concerned about making my intentions of changing my place of residence public knowledge to my roommates, so I kept that small piece of information to myself as I rolled a blunt and listened to them talk about their usual everything and nothing.

    The conversation topic about the latest run-ins with the law or the extremely close calls finally came around, and that was my note to make my move and leave. I didn't really have anywhere in particular to be, but with a phone that for some odd and wonderful reason would never stop singing to me, it only took a few minutes for my next destination to be given to me via a person that had a couple of dollars for me. The thought of ending up at Layla's house every night was not far from the front of my mind, but I pushed it to the side as I took care of The Boy Wonder and Skinny's orders before leaving the house.

    The next couple of hours were filled with the same usual stop here, stop there, stop here stop there that came with my hustle. My personal line always seemed to be in competition with my money line, and that made the monotony of bumping into customers left and right a little more interesting, because for every couple of sells that I made, I got a break in to converse with a beautiful woman that I was either already having sex with or truly working on.

When I finally made it to my new residence, Layla had already unpacked all of the bags that she left with and was laying across the bed watching television. Since I had come home from my extended stay from the free world, the idiot box wasn't something that I indulged in on a regular basis other than playing the X-box. I had spent so many years watching the lives of others and living vicariously through the programming. Layla couldn't understand my sentiment on the subject, but the day that I finally go out I promised myself that I would no longer watch life on a screen. I would live it to the fullest. She must have thought that I would fall right in line with her routine, but after smoking a blunt and getting myself together, I diverted her attention in my direction until she had had enough and went to sleep.

My phone had other plans for me besides sleep, so instead of letting it sing to me until the battery went dead, I chose to answer each and every call. One after the other until I had mapped out a very nice and neat circle that would take me across the city then right back to where I started from. Every call that came after that either had to catch me somewhere on my route or wait until I started another circle.

By the time I decided that I had had enough for the night it was well into the next morning and my morning customers were just starting to make my phone sing. There was something about the loud that made you want to fire it up as soon as you got out of the bed and I couldn't understand it for the life of me. I suffered from the same problem myself, so I completely understood the effect, but the cause was truly lost to me. I guess that's the problem with every drug and its addicts, and loud was no different.

"I hope this ain't gonna be an everyday thing with you" Layla questioned as she passed by me in the hallway on her way to work. "Because I want to see your face right next to mine when I wake up in the morning."

Her words stuck with me for the rest of the day. I wanted to catch a nap for a few minutes, but I went against my first mind and second thought to chase my phone until she got off of work. I couldn't decide what I wanted to do once she made it home, so I played the situation by ear all the way up until she said something that I could take and run with.

Eating has always been one of my necessities that catching a couple of dollars did not come before, and as far as making up for a transgression goes, it has always worked as a great way to make up for doing something wrong. I wasn't sure where I wanted to take her to satisfy that need, but once we got in traffic and she got the chance to tell me about her day and how it went, things started to fall right into place.

   Without having to ask her what she wanted, she told me to only what she had the taste for, but also exactly where she wanted it to come from. And though I didn't frequent the Golden Dragon Chop Suey restaurant because I considered it to be something like a death trap, I had been there before. The food wasn't in my opinion better than John's or Lisa's, but since it wasn't about what I liked or for that matter even what I wanted, I Googled the number and called in her exact order as I made my way to that part of town.

   It didn't surprise me at all that when we got there that the scene was set up for something bad to happen. The dude standing right in front of the building caught my attention immediately, and the fact that he looked extremely suspicious really stuck out to me. Knowing the area and its reputation from my past dealings on that side of the city, I made no attempt to conceal the Smith & Wesson 40 I brought with me. She didn't agree with my decision, but I paid it no mind. My only real concern was to get in and out of the Golden Dragon in the same condition I was in before I stopped there.

He completely understood my silent statement and nodded to make it known as we passed him and came into contact with two more people that were already inside. They gave us a quick once over then returned to their conversation, and that was fine with me. My uncle had told me that "A gun can only protect you if you can get to it", and I completely agreed with his sentiment. I had seen firsthand on more occasions that I care to count a person with a gun get robbed or shot because they couldn't get to it fast enough. I was in no mood to test my quick draw ability or deal with the possibility of that scenario for that matter.

Layla couldn't believe that I kept my gun in my hand until after we got back in the car, but it was what it was. I had learned from experience and the stupidity of others that it is better to pull your gun before you get one pulled on you. And although I tried to explain that fact to her in the simplest terms that I could come up with, she was not buying my explanation. She had her mind made up that my actions were for showing off for her purposes than our personal safety, and it didn't bother me at all.

The thought crossed my mind to tell her that I had used that same set up when I was younger, but I kept it to myself. There was no reason to give her that small piece of information about my past life. Our relationship was based on the facts of our lives at that moment, and I planned to keep it like that for as long as I could. There were so many skeletons in my closet that I tried my best not to venture into that graveyard, and I had no intentions of inviting a visitor.

Halfway back to the house, I changed my mind about eating inside and made a detour to the closest park. The sun was just starting to go down as we finished eating, and I could tell from the look on her face that I had made the right decision. The sun set wasn't anything to be impressed by, but for some odd reason it seemed just a little different than any other that I had seen before it. I figured that it was being in her company that made it special for me, and she felt the same way.

My business line would not stop singing to us, and no matter how much I tried to ignore it, there was something deep inside me that made me keep looking at it. Layla must have been watching me watching my phone because the next time it sung she snatched it off the table and answered it. "Hey now, where you at?"

It truly surprised me that she handled the call in the exact same fashion that I would have, and I was even more impressed that she directed my traffic on the next call in the same way.

"Come on babe, we got a couple of dollars to catch." She explained before getting up and walking towards the truck.

"For real babe?" I called after her completely amazed.

Instead of answering me she just kept walking and I took that as a yes to the question. I wasn't sure who she had talked to or what they wanted, but it didn't bother me at all. My rule of thumb was to always be over prepared just in case the situation called for it, and that went for almost everything that I did including the amount of loud I left the house with.

"Where we headed?" I questioned after I got in the truck and got myself situated.

"I actually don't know." She paused as she looked at my phone. "I told all three people where we were and to call back when they got close."

I was only half listening as she talked my talk on my phone, but I figured that much. She had heard me direct traffic so many times that she probably thought that she could do it without learning how to. I had learned the same lesson myself when I first started out, and ended up having ten people pull up at the same place at the same time, and it turned into a real cluster-fuck. She didn't understand that it was an art to direct traffic, but I didn't hold it against her. The fact that she tried was good enough for me, so I decided to show her how I moved and grooved so she could see for herself that my life was not as simple as he may have thought it was.

Once I got in touch with the people that had called and the new callers, I set up a circle that would take us from where we were, too close to the house. I bent corners and handled business while at the same time explaining to her why I was doing what I was doing. In the back of my mind I thought that she would not be all that interested in the process of selling drugs, but I was wrong. She paid very close attention to the lessons that were being taught to her, and when she didn't understand something she did not hesitate to ask questions.

By the time we made it back to the house, she had completely caught on to what was going on in my life. Her only flaw in the system was the fact that what we were doing was actually against the law, and she was not checking her surroundings for the police first. It was a novice mistake that could cost both of us a lot of freedom, but I was not about to let that happen.

The thought crossed my mind to bring it up to her, but she seemed so excited about what she was doing that I didn't want to rain on her parade with the storms of reality. Plus I could tell that she was extremely turned on from the experience, and I wanted to see exactly what the benefit of that would be for me. Our normal sexual sessions were something special because she gave it her all, so I knew that the rest of the night would probably be well worth keeping my mouth shut and my thoughts to myself.

Chapter Twelve

As I read the text message from Cuzzo, the thought actually crossed my mind to ignore it. I hadn't seen or talked to him in almost a month, and it didn't bother me at all. His offer to buy me a drink seemed like a set up for something else. He always had an ulterior motive behind everything he did, and I knew that from not only firsthand experience, but also from the outside looking in. I figured that he had to have something up his sleeve that he wanted from me, so instead of agreeing outright I left the possibility open and continued with my day.

My phone seemed to be trying to set a record for the most calls received in a day, and I was not bothered by it at all. As a matter of fact, I had an appointment set up to meet with B when he got off work and I needed every odd nickel and dime I could come up with to spend on my purchase.

Twenty here, thirty there, fifty here, forty there; the sells just kept coming and it seemed like everything was going almost exactly how I wanted it to. In the back of my mind though, I had the thought that for every step I took forward there was always the couple of steps backwards that went with it, but the calls just kept coming and wouldn't allow me the chance to dwell on it for too long. I knew that there was nothing that I could say or anything that could be done to change it no matter how I felt, so I pushed the negative thoughts from my mind and got back to business. Fifty, here, a hundred there, thirty here twenty there.

When Layla got off of work she called to check in on me, and the interruption was well received. I needed a break from the monotony of running back and forth chasing after my phone, so I directed the next two calls in the general direction of the apartment. After taking care of their orders, I pulled up and went in the house.

"Babe you hungry?" Layla questioned as soon as I walked through the door.

"Always momma." I responded as I checked the locks on the front door then tossed my bag on the couch as I headed for the kitchen.

"What you want?" She shot back.

Several things crossed my mind in response to her question, but none of them had anything to do with food. As a matter of fact, as I stared at her as she stood in front of the refrigerator with the door open, she looked like the best thing on the menu.

I know exactly what I want to eat." I paused to run my arm across the kitchen table knocking everything on the floor. Come here girl and feed me!"

I could tell from the look in her eyes that she knew exactly what I had in mind. She started to say something in response but instead of speaking she caught herself and followed my instruction. I wasn't sure if the kitchen table was sturdy enough to support my idea, but I was so caught up in the moment it didn't matter to me one way or the other. She must have had something like the same thought, because before I could ask her about it, she hopped up on it. And after getting her out of her clothes without any dispute from her or the table I got the answer that I was looking for.

My first thought when I got myself situated in between her legs was to do what I normally did when I found myself in that situation, but it just didn't feel right. For some odd reason something inside of me was telling me that something was truly missing. I wasn't too sure what exactly it was, but as I looked around the room the thought came to me, so I got up and opened the freezer door and grabbed a tray of ice cubes.

"What you think you gonna do with that?" She questioned as I cracked the tray and removed a piece of ice.

"You'll see baby." I responded before tossing the ice in my mouth.

Holding the ice in my mouth, I used it as I kissed the inside of her thighs. I could tell from her reaction I was driving her crazy, and that only made it even better for me. The cold sensations followed by the hot ones coming from my own body temperature did something extreme for her. I wasn't sure if it was the alternating feeling of hot and cold or just the feeling of my cunnilingus that had her shaking uncontrollably, but I did know from her reaction to a brief pause that I made to get another piece of ice, that she was really enjoying herself.

I could hear my phone singing in the other room, but I paid it no mind. I had started something already between Layla's legs that I couldn't just get up and walk away from without it being a problem, and it didn't bother me at all. Plus she had started to give me instructions on where to go and how hard or soft she want it, so I figured that she was getting close to the point of orgasm.

More to the left here. A little harder there. A little more tongue here. More sucking there. And just when I got where she wanted me to be her body started to shake. It started from her legs and worked its way up her body until the ear piercing, room shaking scream that accompanied her orgasm arrived.

The first time that it had happened it took me by complete surprise. I had had the pleasure to experience all kinds of weird and colorful reactions that were attributed to the female climax due to the plethora of women that I had been with, but even that didn't matter. Layla's orgasms had such a powerful effect on her body that just having one took all of the energy that she could muster, and for some odd reason to say that she was vocal about it would be a true understatement. Her screams could be heard by anyone and everyone who happened to be anywhere close to the vicinity.

The thought crossed my mind to tell her how much I really enjoyed her orgasms, but I kept it to myself. There was no reason to give her something that she would probably use against me if the need ever arose. Her response to climaxing was one of the most beautiful things that I had ever had the pleasure to witness and be a part of, and though I didn't react accordingly to show

how I really felt about it, I still felt it in a way that I couldn't completely understand.

Now that what I call a snack baby!" I laughed as I leaned against the kitchen wall and admired her laid out on the table.

"Why you do that to me?" She questioned almost out of breath.

"I was hungry." I responded.

"Hungry or horny babe?" She shot back.

"Probably a little bit of both." I paused to close the distance between us. "As a matter of fact, definitely both." I answered before giving her a kiss.

My lust had gotten the better of me for a few minutes while I enjoyed the taste of Layla, but the thought of my appointment with my supplier was not completely forgotten. So much so, that after admiring my handy oral work for a few more minutes, my thought got right back on business immediately.

Babe, I'm gonna shake. If you need me or anything else, you know how to reach out and touch me." I explained before walking out of the door.

My business line had not stopped singing while I was enjoying myself with Layla, but that didn't surprise me at all. I had come to the realization that my hustle did not come with a set work schedule or the hours that came with a legal job. I had heard somewhere that drug dealing is one of the hardest occupations to have because of the hours and the consequences, and I couldn't agree more, but it didn't stop me from doing it.

    I had missed B's call but he sent me a text message with an alternate time and location to meet him, and that worked out perfect for me. My stash was starting to run a little low, and that was not a good look for my business venture. The supply and demand idea depended only on if my supply could cover the demand of my customers, and until I went back to the store to replenish my stock, I would not be in business for too much longer if I continued to answer my phone. The thought crossed my mind to say something to B about stepping out to join me for a drink as he counted my money up for my purchase, but I kept it to myself. I was more concerned about the fact that the bag I was buying was off by four and a half grams, so we had that discussion instead. My rule of thumb has always been that I have to get my money's worth when I buy something, and a short was completely unacceptable when I was paying for it.

After the business was taken care of, I made a quick stop at my storage unit to drop off the majority of my bag because I didn't need it. I never kept product where I laid my head, and since I had moved in with Layla, I couldn't keep it there. I only brought out what I thought I would need for a day or two, and then I got back in traffic.

By the time my phone slowed down, I was actually hungry. The snack that I had devoured earlier did not do anything to fill me up, but it did taste good. I couldn't make up my mind on exactly what I wanted to eat to satisfy my appetite, so I stopped at the next place that I passed by. Rally's is not my first choice when I have one, but I figured that it would have to do until something else better came along.

"I wonder who the fuck that is?" I asked myself as my phone signaled that I had a new text message. Cuzzo had asked me to step out and have a drink with him, so it didn't surprise me at all that it was him checking in to see if I was still stepping out. I didn't have anything else planned for the evening, but that didn't mean anything. I knew that he wanted something, I just couldn't make up my mind if I wanted to go see what it was.

After leaving the drive thru and bending a couple of corners to make a delivery I was right around the corner from my house. The thought crossed my mind to pull up and just get whatever it was that he wanted out of the way, but my personal line interrupted my train of thought. I figured that it was Layla calling to inform me that she was in need of something, but when I looked at the screen I seen it was Latoya. I hadn't spoken to her for almost a week for some reason or another, and I knew that if I answered the phone she would not be pleased with me, but I went against my first mind and accepted the call. "Hey now babe, what's shaking?"

"Day, if you don't come fuck me then we breaking up." She answered in her most serious tone.

"Yes, ma'am, I'm pulling up." I responded before ending the call dropping the phone back in my lap.

"I guess it don't matter what you want Cuzzo." I said to myself as I drove right passed my street. Latoya lived right around the corner from me, so I turned on the next street and pulled right up just like I had said I would.

When Latoya opened her front door the look on her face was a mixture of happy and mad mixed together, but I paid it no mind as I stood on the front porch and returned her stare. I hadn't planned on coming to see her, but I didn't want the problems that would come from being on their bad side. Plus I had no intentions of breaking up with her under any circumstances because of our mutual love of women. She also didn't have a problem with my lifestyle and that was hard to find in a woman.

"Girl get out of the way and let Day in Bitch. "A voice called from inside the house.

"I wasn't sure who was talking, but as I walked inside of the house and seen Jody lying across the couch. I was truly pleasantly surprised. I hadn't seen her since I first met Latoya, but I still remembered the experience. It was one that I will probably never forget because Jody was just as good in bed if not better than Latoya was, and she loved fellatio in a way that I had only seen on rare occasions.

"I thought you said you wanted me to come fuck you?" I paused to look at Jody. "Did I miss something?"

"Nope you got it right Day." Latoya answered.

"And when you finished fucking her, I want you to fuck me." Jody cut in.

"So let me get this straight. If I don't fuck you Latoya we breaking up right?" I questioned just to get a clear understanding.

"That's right." She shot back.

"And what's gonna happen if I don't fuck you Jody?" I asked just out of pure curiosity.

"I'm not gonna give you this pussy and head ever again. And i'm more fun one on one. She explained.

The thought crossed my mind to say something clever back to her, but due to the fact that I had never had her in a one on one situation, I kept my thought to myself. If she was any better all by herself than she was with Latoya to give her a little assistance. I refused to do anything to mess that up. If she wanted to watch first then fight second that didn't bother me at all. I only had one other concern after I got a crystal clear understanding of how the rest of my night was going to play itself out.

"When I'm finished with both of you bitches one on one just promise me that y'all gonna jump on me, cause I love a two on one fight." I explained.

Chapter Thirteen

"I wonder who the fuck that is?" I asked myself as the singing of my phone woke me up. I had thought that I had heard it sing once before that, but I just blamed it on the fact that it always sung, Latoya and Jody had fought as hard as they could together after I finished them off one on one, and I couldn't be mad at the results. It just seemed to me that I had just closed my eyes to go to sleep and my phone started singing to me.

"This better be somebody I really fuck wit." I told my phone as I grabbed it off of the bed and accepted the call. "Hey now."

"Bro them people just kick in yo spot. The caller informed me.

"What people?" I questioned.

"The alphabet boys pimp." He answered.

"Which letters?" I shot back.

"F-E-D." He responded.

"Good looking pimp." I thanked him ending the call.

The thought crossed my mind to all types of things that wouldn't help me, but I pushed them from my mind as I called Layla to see if the Feds had paid her a visit also. She was still asleep and completely unaware about what I was talking about, so I ended the call with her and threw my phone back on the bed.

"What you doing Day?" Jody questioned as I entered her from behind. "You ain't get enough?"

"Them people just kicked my house in." I explained as I woke Latoya back up to join us. "I can't say if I'm going to get too many more chances to do this before I go on vacation again."

"Well get this pussy." She responded as she pushed back to meet my thrust.

Latoya fell right in line with what was going on and I enjoyed both of them all over again before I got out of the bed. I couldn't make up my mind what I wanted to do once I got myself together, so I smoked a blunt all by myself and let my mind run through scenarios and possibilities.

When I finally finished thinking the whole of my situation through, I sent Latoya and Jody around the corner to my house to check the scene and report back. I knew that there was nothing that I could do to change the situation for the better by going to see what was going on myself, so I waited patiently for her to call me and give me all of the information that I needed to make my next move.

"Something told me not to pull up on them niggas." I thought to myself. Several thoughts ran through my mind as I waited and not one of them had anything to do with what had happened. The consequences of my actions meant nothing to me because I had already come to grips with what the outcome could be. I also knew that I would only be a matter of time before I found out in which direction things would turn, so when my phone rung, I was prepared for the worst while silently hoping for the best.

"Day they got Shoota laid out in the front yard and he looks like they beat the shit out of him." Latoya paused for a split second. "And all of your neighbors are outside watching the festivities.

"Shoota the only person you see? They ain't got nobody else?" I questioned.

"Yeah Skinny in the back of one of the cars, but I don't see Cuzzo nowhere, his car not even out here." She answered.

"Ok. Babe bring y'all ass back ASAP. And make sure you get a good count on all the police cares you pass on the way." I explained before ending our call.

"Something ain't right." I thought to myself as I called Cuzzo from the house phone. I couldn't understand how Skinny and Shoota were there but he wasn't. When he answered the phone it caught me by surprise, but I kept it to myself as I gave him the rundown about what was going on at my house.

I made sure that I didn't talk to him for too long to ensure that the call was not being traced, but I made sure that I got my point across and a couple of my questions answered before I hung up.

"Babe there are three cars, two trucks, and a big ass van in between my house and yours." Latoya explained when she walked through the door.

"I expected more than that." I responded.

"Boy are you serious?" Jody cut in. "What the fuck have y'all done?"

The thought crossed my mind to explain the whole situation to her so she would have a good understanding about what was going on, but I decided against it. The truth wouldn't change anything, and I also knew for a fact that the less somebody knew about you the less they could tell if the opportunity presented itself.

"I ain't did shit babe. I was here with y'all and I'm so glad I was." I responded as I looked out of the front door window to see if they were followed back home by the police.

"Well what you gonna do?" Latoya questioned.

"I'm gonna do what I usually do when situations like this arise babe. I'm gonna get money and enjoy life to the fullest." I answered.

"What if the police try to stop you?" Jody inquired.

"They gonna have to do their job, because I'll be good God-damned if I don't do mine." I paused to grab my goodie bag off the floor." I gonna get in traffic, so I'm gonna need you hoes to pray for me." I finished as I walked out the front door.

When I got inside of my car, I silently thanked God that there was another way to get away from Latoya's house that didn't pass by my house. I wasn't sure if the police knew what kind of car I was in because I had stopped going home and hanging out with anybody that stopped by my house, but I didn't want to take any chances either. The last thing I needed was to get into a chase with them people before I got a few things taken care of, so as I made the turn to take the back way out of our subdivision I acted as if nothing was wrong.

I didn't really have anywhere special to be, but I just felt more comfortable on the move. Latoya's house was too close to what was going on for my taste, and as soon as I put several block between us, for some odd reason I felt better. The thought crossed my mind to go to Layla's house to lay low for a few minutes while I put my complete plan together, but I knew that she was there asleep and I was not ready to explain my actions or have the conversation that I knew would come along with that explanation.

""Oh shit. Here comes the bullshit." I said to myself as I looked at my personal phone screen and seen that it was my parole officer calling me. I was not scheduled to see her for another two months, but I figured that since the police were at my house and they brought an extremely large amount of backup that she was aware of the situation. The thought crossed my mind to not answer the phone, but I decided against it because I knew that she would keep calling until I did. "Hey now Miss Steph, what can I do for you?"

"Mr. Smith I need to see you, are you busy?" She questioned.

"Not really busy, but what you need?" I responded.

"Nothing really. I just need you to fill out some paperwork for your life." She answered.

"What kind of paperwork Miss Steph? Can't it wait 'til my schedule appointment?" I questioned.

"No Mr. Smith this needs to be taken care of as soon as possible." She answered.

The thought crossed my mind to play along with what she was saying, but that didn't really make sense to me. I wasn't positive that she knew about my house being visited by law enforcement, but I had the idea on my mind and that was all that mattered to me. Plus we had always spoken honestly in our past dealings, so I decided to go with that and see where it got me.

"If I come see you Miss Steph I'm going to jail ain't I?" I questioned.

"What makes you ask that?" She responded.

"Come on lady keep it real with me." I shot back.

"Yes. If you come in you are going to jail. For what I don't know, but you will find out when you get here. "She answered.

"Well, when you got up this morning and put your suit on, you went to work to do your job. When them people put on their uniforms, badges, and guns and reported for duty, they went to work to do they job. And when I put on my clothes and got myself together, I'm ready to work and I'm gonna do my job. So if y'all want me y'all gonna have to do y'all jobs better than I do mine. Have a nice day Miss Steph." I finished before I ended the call and dropped the phone in my lap.

I figured that I would probably be going back to jail after I answered my phone and got the news that the alphabet boys were at my house, but after talking to my parole officer, I knew it for a fact. Her confirmation of what I was thinking cleared up more than one issue that I was having with my situation and that was all I really needed.

Going to jail was not a new thing for me, but what I didn't have the first two times was a little time to plan for the trip. Not being at my house was a blessing that I couldn't be happier about. It rubbed me the wrong way that Shoota and Skinny went down, but there was nothing that I could do about their situation, so I pushed it from my mind and started putting my plan together for my next set of moves. My business line must have known that I needed every dime that I could get my hands on, because as soon as I thought about putting up some money it started singing to me."Hey now."

Chapter Fourteen

"Day be careful today if you leave this house." Layla paused to give me a kiss. "I had a dream that them people was chasing you and I have a sixth sense for them type of things" She explained as she walked out of the room.

The thought crossed my mind to respond to what she had said, but before I could I heard the front door close. I took it as a sign that I didn't need to say anything to her about how she felt, so I just made a mental note of her warning before I rolled back over and went back to sleep

When I woke back up my business line had several missed calls and a few missed texts. It didn't surprise me, so instead of being in a rush to deal with them I took my time to get myself together before leaving the house to go to work. Layla's warning played in my mind for the first hour that I weaved in and out of traffic and it made me feel some type of way. I wasn't sure if it was fear or paranoia the kept tapping me on my shoulder and making me super aware of my surroundings and the cars that I seen on the streets, but after two blunts I finally calmed down and got into the groove of things.

In my mind it didn't matter if I wanted to or not, because if I got caught doing what I was doing I was going to jail anyway so it really didn't matter all that much. My plan was to put as much money as I could up before my luck ran out. My uncle told me one day that "hustlers have to be lucky everyday them people only have to get lucky once", and those words of wisdom stuck with me like glue since they rolled off of his tongue.

The conversation that I had with Layla after I finally let her in on the fact that the police had visited my residence went much better than I thought it would. I figured that she would not want anything else to do with me after that fact became known, but it was just the opposite. She informed me that she was not going anywhere and that I was stuck with her for as long as I wanted her. That caught me off guard for a split second, but after digesting the information I took it with a grain of salt because I had heard that before from an ex before I went on my first vacation and it didn't work out anywhere close to how she said it would.

"I need to pull on Craig." I told myself after I made the last delivery to complete the circle that I had started. I hadn't seen my lawyer since I gave him ten thousand to retain his services for when I got caught. It was a part of the lifestyle that I chose to live so it was an expense that needed to be taken care of. Death and jail were all that I had to look forward to on the negative side, so I kept my lawyer on my speed dial and an insurance policy paid up just in case anything went wrong. I really didn't have anything special to say to Craig when I walked into his office, so our conversation only lasted a few minutes. I wasn't there when they kicked in and I didn't have the slightest idea of what they took out of the house, so I didn't really have too much information to give. He was only concerned with the facts and since I didn't have many, he let me know that he would check into it and get back with me with the few answer that he could come up with. He also let me know that until I got caught his services were not needed and that I should go about my life until that time came and then give him a call.

"That's why I fuck with him." I thought to myself as I got back into traffic. The few minutes that I spent chit chatting with him about my situation gave my business line a chance to set up another circle for me and that was exactly what I needed. My personal line kept up as usual but for some odd reason I wasn't as interested in attending to it as I usually was. Those were chances to run into them people that didn't pay for my time, so I was picky about who I stopped by to see.

The plan that I put into place depended on the people that I had around me and what they would do when I wasn't around. Layla promised that she would hold me down when I got caught, but that was not something that I believed wholeheartedly. I wanted to more than I wanted not to, but I wouldn't be sure about that until the time came and it would be too late if I was wrong to do something about it, so I planned to be prepared either way.

I had more women in my life than I cared to count, but some of them were only occasional sexual partners. A few were regular sexual partners, and only a hand full were on my all the time list. I had talked to the chosen few that I dealt with regardless of the situation about my situation, and all of them were on board for what I had planned. I wasn't sure if all of them would live up to their promises and declarations, but it didn't matter. All I really needed from them was the start up loyalty to get me through the first stages of my vacation, and everything else would take care of itself. If they lasted that long I would be alright even if they didn't have the insight to see me through to the end, and that was all that was important to me.

Latoya, Y, Moet, and Diosa all played a part in my life one way or another that had nothing to do with our sexual dealings, and that came in very handy for what I had up my sleeve. I knew that they were not friends in the normal sense of the word, but since they all knew about each other from my honestly in my relationships they were all on speaking terms. That was all that I needed from them towards each other when the time came for them to come into play, and I set it up so everybody had everybody's number so it wouldn't be hard for me to reach out and touch whoever I needed when I needed them.

My business line continued to sing to me and the calls were well received. The proceeds from my hustle that I usually spent on whatever it was that caught my eye was now since everything went south being put to the side. I also made every middle-man move that I could add extras to that stash. The odds that somebody would jump ship when everything went south were very good regardless of how I felt about it, so I decided that I would not put all of my eggs in one basket because it didn't make sense. I figured that the more that I had in different places, the better chance I had to be able to get to it when the time arose.

"I wonder who gonna jump ship first?" I asked myself as I guesstimated how much money I had put up between them. I had just as much if not more in Layla's care and with each call it continued to grow. My personal living expenses were still something that I had to take care of, so I started to move a little more than I usually did to make sure that all of my ends met exactly where they were supposed to. I wasn't sure how much money I would need or exactly how long I would be gone this time around, but I figured that the more I had in escrow the more I could do when I needed it, and that thought pushed me forward.

I also had a couple of other women that were part of my team, but they played such a small part that I didn't bother to let them in on what was going on. I wasn't sure of their loyalty when it came to holding on to money for me in the first place, so I kept the out of the loop and the drop off rotation. It didn't make sense to me to just give my money away for no reason regardless of how good the sex was or how many times they professed their love for me. I needed to know for sure how trustworthy they were before I went in that direction and I planned to find out before I took the chance.

"Hey now Day, Where you at in the world?" Jessica questioned after answering her phone.

"I'm in traffic babe. Where you at?" I responded.

I'm at home chilling, pull up on me." She answered.

"I got a couple of stops to make then I'm gonna do just that, so be outside." I explained before ending the call and dialing another number.

"Day what's good my dude?" Ne Ne questioned after answering the phone.

"Shit in traffic. Where you at in the world?" I shot back.

"I'm in traffic too, so where you wanna meet up at?" She inquired.

"Meet me at Jessica's house ASAP." I answered.

Be there in ten babe and I got a couple of dollars for you too." She informed me.

"Good looking. One." I responded before ending the call.

"I wonder how this gonna turn out?" I asked myself as I pulled up to my first stop. Jessica and Ne Ne were friends that I had met through one of my other female customers when I first started out, and I ended up dealing with both of them on more than a business level. They didn't have a problem with me seeing and doing both of them from the beginning, and that worked out perfectly for me. It also worked well that they seen each other in-between their other relationships which was a plus that I hadn't planned on, but I enjoyed it every time the thought crossed my mind or the time permitted it.

By the time I made it to Jessica's house they were both sitting on the front porch. I knew what I wanted to do, but I didn't have the slightest idea about how I was going to pull it off. I couldn't just come right out and tell them that I wanted to test their loyalty to me because I knew that it wouldn't work out like I wanted it to. But I also didn't want to keep them all the way in the dark about what I was doing, so I ran several solutions to my problem through my mind before I got out of the car.

"What's on yo mind Day?" Ne Ne questioned as I walked up the steps.

"I hope he just wanna smoke and fuck." Jessica cut in. "Cause that's what I got on my mind."

The thought crossed my mind to forget what I had planned so that I could fall right in line with what Jessica was talking about, but I let it pass. I knew that option would be available after our conversation, so I got my thoughts back focused on the task at hand.

"I know you heard me Day." Ne Ne said before I responded.

"Yeah babe I heard you. And yes Jessica I definitely heard you. But before I address your idea I got an idea I wanna run past y'all right fast." I responded.

Our conversation only took a couple of minutes to have, and they were both down for my idea. There wasn't even a question raised about why I wanted to leave a few things with them that I didn't want touched. I thought twice about going through with it as I looked both of them over, because I didn't want to have to cut them loose if anything went wrong, but I stuck to it. It was going to be what it was regardless of how I felt about them on the flip-side of the coin, so after we finished talking, I spent the next hour taking Jessica up on her offer with Ne Ne assisting in every way that I needed her to.

When I finished with them and finally got back to business it was already dark outside. Time seemed to fly while I was trying to put both of them down, and I wasn't bothered by it at all. Layla was working overtime so instead of heading back to the house I continued to answer my phone until I needed to refill my bag. I figured that I had brought enough out of the storage to keep me moving for a couple of days, but I was wrong. That didn't bother me at all because I needed to do all that I could before I was in the position that I couldn't do anything.

After stopping to re-up and checking to see how much inventory I still had to work with, I resumed my business dealings. Money motivated me to stay out longer and handle as many calls as possible, and Layla understood. She informed me that she didn't agree with my business plan, but she understood why I was doing what I was doing. That was all that I could ask of her, so after she texted me to let me know that she was getting off, I took a few more calls, then headed in for the night.

Strangely I made it to the house before she did, so I ran her bath water and lit a few candles to set the mood. I wasn't sure if she would be interested in what I had in mind, but it didn't matter to me. I hadn't played the game for more than an hour straight since my situation had changed, and if all else failed I knew that I could enjoy a few hours of Call of Duty to keep me entertained.

Layla must have been thinking along the same lines that I was, because after she got out of the tub, she was more than ready for a sexual session that lasted until well after the sun came back up.

That was right up my alley, and I enjoyed my time with and in her like I did every time the opportunity presented itself. She was tired from working a double shift, but she put her best foot forward and kept up with me as best as she could until she couldn't take it anymore.

The thought crossed my mind to leave her alone after she fell asleep, but it only lasted a few minutes. I had more energy than I knew what to do with for some odd reason, and my stomach was talking to me. I didn't see any reason to bother her at that moment to satisfy my hunger, so I made a call to Debbie's Delight to order breakfast, and left to go pick it up.

I made it there without anything going wrong, but on the way back home I found myself being followed by a marked St. Louis City police car. I paid it no mind for the first few blocks that it was behind me, because I wasn't doing anything wrong or even headed in that direction. After it followed me through two turns that I made to get back on the highway to head home, my interest in the car started to pique. So much so that when he turned his lights on to signal me to pull over, I was already prepared to run.

"Here we go again." I said to myself as I put my foot on the gas.

Chapter Fifteen

"Baby when you gonna get my name tattooed on you?" Layla questioned as she lay across the bed and watched me play the game.

The thought crossed my mind to make up the best lie that I could come up with to pacify her, but it didn't last long. She had proven to me on more than one occasion that she was really in my corner when I needed her, and I couldn't deny it. The thought had crossed my mind on more than one occasion to do just that, but I had never gone through with it.

"Babe did you hear me?" When you gone get my name tattooed on you?" She questioned again.

"I don't know babe, that's a major step in our relationship. Are you sure you ready for that?" I shot back.

"You stuck with me now, so make that shake for me like you do everything else I ask you." She responded as she got out of the bed and walked out of the room.

"That lady crazy." I thought to myself as I continued to play the game waiting on my phone to sing. It only took a few minutes for the calls to start coming in, and as soon as I got my circle mapped out I turned off the game and left the house.

The first lap took me to the other side of the city and back, but my next trip took me in a different direction and I followed where my phone took me. I had not got a call from KK in a few days, but when his number popped up on my phone I took a double take at it before I answered. "Hey now."

"I'm at the shop dirty, pull up on me." He said.

"Give me fifteen minutes pimp." I responded before ending the call.

"This must be fate." I said to myself as I made my way to Ink Doctor Tattoo shop. I had two stops to make before I got there, and the next three calls I directed in that direction. I wasn't sure why I felt strangely as I pulled up on the parking lot, but for some odd reason I did.

I waiteded in my car until all of my other business was taken care of, before I got out of the car and entered the shop. Dealing with KK had brought me to the Ink Doctor on more occasions than I could recall, but the thought to get a tattoo while I was there never crossed my mind.

After taking care of KK's order. I took a few minutes to look around the shop. There were two or three people sitting in the waiting area, and all of them looked nervous for some odd reason. The clerk sitting at the front desk just spun around in his chair and he looked like he was getting paid to do nothing.

"Day you ain't never stayed in here this long. You thinking about getting some more work done?" KK questioned as I looked over the pictures on the wall.

"Yes and no pimp." I responded.

"What you got in mind?" He shot back.

"My bitch wants me to get her name on me." I answered.

"What about you other bitches?" He paused. "What they gonna say?"

"That's a damn good question." I admitted.

The thought crossed my mind to let the thought go of getting Layla's name tattooed on me, but as soon as I tried she called me. "Hey now."

"Babe where you at?" She questioned.

"I'm at the Ink Doctor." I answered.

"So you gonna take care of that for me huh?" She shot back with a hint of excitement in her voice.

"What the fuck have I gotten myself into?" I thought to myself before responding to her question. "Yeah babe, why not? As a matter of fact pull up on me."

"Ok. Give me fifteen minutes." She said.

"One." I finished before ending the call.

The thought crossed my mind to call Layla back and tell her not to come because I had changed my mind, but before I could my phone rang again. "Hey now Latoya."

"Where you at in the world?" She questioned.

"At the Ink Doctor gettin Layla's name tattooed on me." I answered.

"What about me Day?" She shot back.

"What are you talking about?" I questioned.

"When you finished getting her name on you. I want mines on your ass too! That's what I mean." She answered.

"Ok. Fuck it. Pull up on me." I instructed.

"I'm on my way." She informed me.

"One." I finished before ending the call and answering the call that was incoming. "Hey now Moet."

After talking to her and getting the same response that I got from Latoya, I figured that I was in trouble. It didn't make any sense to me to get Layla, Latoya, and Moet's name on me and leave out Y and DIosa. The all held a place in my heart, and it seemed unfair to get one or two and not get them all, so I made the calls and let them know where I was and what I had up my sleeve.

"This could get extremely interesting." I explained to KK as I let him know what I had planned.

"Are you sure this how you wanna play it?" He questioned after hearing my idea.

"Yep." I answered.

"Well, where you gonna put six bitches names on you?" He paused to shake his head. "Cause no matter where you put them somebody gone feel some type of way about not getting a different spot. Trust me I know."

I hadn't put too much thought into where I was going to put them, but as soon as he finished talking to me, the idea of the perfect place popped right into my head. It made sense in more ways than one, and even if somebody complained about it wouldn't really matter because none of them would be last.

"On my side pimp. I'm gonna put all of them on my ribs." I paused as I let the thought sink in. God made Eve from Adam's rib so it makes sense in the world to me to get them all on my side."

"So they will always be by yo side huh?" KK cut in.

"Hell yeah. That too." I agreed.

I wasn't sure how my plan of having them come to the shop to watch me get their names tattooed on me would work out, but I prayed for the best. The only person I couldn't be completely sure about was Layla, and for some odd reason she stopped by to check it out before anybody else even pulled up.

Latoya walked in while her name was being done and didn't say a word until it was finished. Moet, Y, and Diosa pulled up within minutes of each other, and nobody caused a scene. It was weird to have all of them in the same room together, but it didn't seem wrong.

When their names were done all of them left and went their separate ways. I still had one more name to get, and I knew that no matter how much I wanted her to see it, that would not be possible. My ex wife hated my guts for whatever reason she had, and I was fine with it. There was nothing that I could do to change it, and even if I could I probably wouldn't.

"Oh shit." KK mumbled as he finished the name on the bottom of my list.

"What's wrong pimp?" I questioned.

"You'll see." He responded as a female walked into his booth with both of us.

She was pregnant and I could tell that she wasn't happy about something. There was also something extremely familiar about her, but I just couldn't put my finger on what it was. I let my mind run to see if I could figure it out, but when I couldn't, I went with my first mind on those issues.

"Excuse me lil momma, but don't I know you?" I inquired.

"Yes you do. I'm your ex-wife's niece." She answered.

"Now that's crazy, cause I just got her name tattooed on me, and I knew that she would never see it or know about it, but I guess God has proved me wrong." I explained.

"He has as he always will." She paused to look at KK. "But if you don't mind, can I borrow him for a minute?"

When KK returned from his conversation with my ex's niece he informed me that he was the father of her child, and that he had made a mistake that he could not correct. I completely understood where he was coming from due to the fact that I had made one of my own with another member of the family, so we had something in common there.

So much so, that after putting the final touches on my tattoo, he refused to accept my money for his work. He rationalized it as I had already been through enough pain dealing with that family, and that he might need me in the future. I couldn't argue with that at all, so after I got wrapped up I got right back in traffic.

"That's crazy." I thought to myself as I thought about how my ex would find out about her name being on my body. My business line only let me dwell on the thought for a few seconds before it started to sing to me.

The time that I had spent getting tattooed had given my call log a chance to get backed up, so I spent the rest of my day trying to get caught up. The calls seemed to keep coming along with the ones that I already had waiting for, so I kept busy without having to put too much effort into it.

Everybody permanently etched into my skin called or texted to check on me at one point, and it amused me to no end. Moet was the first to say something about her placement on my side, but I paid her no mind because there was nothing that I could do about it at that point in time. What was done was done, and she had to live with it just as I did.

By the time I made it back to the house, Layla was laying across the bed watching something on the television. I had no real interest in her choice of programming, so I turned the game on the other TV. I had a few calls lined up for me to run into, but until I go a few more I planned to entertain myself with some Call of Duty.

"Baby, let me see you side. Do it still hurt?" She questioned.

The thought crossed my mind to avoid showing her my tattoo after I got the other names added after hers, but she had other plans for me. I wasn't sure how she would take it even though she knew about every other woman that I had in my life, but I realized that it was too late to worry about it at that moment, so I dropped the joystick and lifted up my shirt.

"What the fuck did you do Day?" She screamed. Nigga I said to get my name tattooed on you not every bitch you fuck with.

I didn't have anything to say in response, so I picked the joystick back up, and continued to play the game.

"Answer my question Day. What the fuck did you do? As a matter of fact, just tell me why you did it."

Now that was something altogether different, so I took a few minutes to give her a quick rundown about why I did what I did.

My reasoning actually had something logical behind it whether she agreed or not, so after I finished with my explanation, she just shook her head.

"So how am I any more special than any of them other bitches you got on you?" She questioned.

"Did you really look at it babe?" I shot back.

"No." She answered.

"Well you might wanna take a look so you can see how you are separated from the rest." I paused to life my shirt back up. "Now look, because that crossed my mind too.

"Is that a number 1 after my name boy?" She laughed. "So I'm number one to you baby?"

"Without a doubt babe." I answered.

"I better be nigga. And you bet not ever forget it." She said before lying back down and returning to her program that had come back on after the commercial break.

"Now that was a close call." I thought to myself, because when I played that scenario out in my mind after leaving the shop, it played out with more screaming and a lot more violence. Layla never ceased to amaze me with her reactions to the things that I did, and that situation was not different. She proved to me why she was my number one, and if she continued with that type of behavior we would last for a long time.

Chapter Sixteen

"Babe I keep having this dream that you gonna get locked up." Layla informed me as I played the game.

"Ok. Babe." I responded.

"No nigga you not listening. Do you think that you tore that pretty ass truck up running from them people by accident?" She questioned.

"Yeah I do." I paused to drop the joystick and turn to face her. "I actually blame it on the bitch that didn't pull to the side of the road when she seen all them God-damn police lights. If you asking me, but it is what it is."

"I don't care what you say, when you leave this house I want you ass to be careful. I keep telling you that I'm clairvoyant." She explained.

The thought crossed my mind to start an argument with her about the depth of her clairvoyance, but I decided against it. I was in no mood to travel down that road with her on any subject, because winning was something that she tried to do in everything that she did. Sex was the only thing that I let her.

"Ok babe. I got you." I shot back.

My business line had been singing since I got out of the bed, but I was in no rush to deal with it. My body hurt all over from the accident that I had been in a couple of days before. It cost me the truck, but that didn't matter to me. It was not the first vehicle that I had destroyed in a high speed police chase, and in my mind I was certain that it would not be the last.

The only thing that was important to me was getting away, and as long as that happened I had no issue with what had happened before that. My uncle always told me that it was easier to get a car out of the impound than it was go get a nigga out of jail and I believed him wholeheartedly.

I mean it Day. But if you get in trouble I better be the first person you call. You see how fast I got there to get yo ass last time?" She asked.

"Come on babe, I hear you. You just beating a dead horse, please let it go. As a matter of fact I'm out of here I'll get with you later." I explained as I grabbed my bag and headed for the door.

"Hold up Day. Give me that gun. I want you to come right back." She called after me.

That was not something that I did on a regular basis, and it definitely was not something that I planned to go along with, but before I made it out of the door she was right behind me.

"I'm not playing with you. Give me that gun, you don't need it." She paused to put out her hand. "Put it right there." The thought crossed my mind to just walk out of the door, but it didn't last long. She had held me down every time that I needed her to, and that meant a lot to me. I was not truly comfortable parting ways with my firearm, but I had a trick up my sleeve so I handed her the gun off my side without any argument.

"You must think I'm stupid huh Day?" She questioned after taking the gun from my hand. "Give me the other one in yo back pocket."

"This bitch good." I mumbled under my breath as I handed her the other gun. I didn't know that she even seen me get it out, but I couldn't be mad at her about it either way. Not being armed was a major no-no in my occupation so staying in traffic was not a part of my plan anymore. It went right out of the window when my other gun left my possession.

I had several stops to make that I had set up in the circle that I plotted, but without some form of protection with me anything that wasn't a quick hand to hand was out of the question. The fact that I always had something or another with me would get me through any of them without any issue, but anything other than that was a risk that I refused to take.

By the time I made it halfway through my circle, Miser had called me back to bump into him. He was running a little short on his bag and needed something to get him through until he went back to the store. I had gotten used to that from him because my supplier was better than his, so we worked it out as best as we could. I had two more stops to make before I got to him, so I let him know where to meet me, and then got back to business.

On my way to my next stop I received a call from one of my smoking buddies wanting to spend some time with me while I was out. Her house was right on my route, so I stopped by and picked her up to ride along while I handled my business. The fact that she enjoyed giving fellatio while I drove was also a plus and actually the only reason I agreed to let her accompany me.

As I pulled up to the last stop on my circle something caught my attention out of the corner of my eye. I wasn't sure what it was at first, but after taking a second to get a better look in that direction, I noticed that it was a couple of marked police cars blocking a car in down the street. That did not sit well with me at all because of my situation and I knew that I could not afford to be stopped for any reason.

"There go them people Day, what you gonna do?" My passenger questioned as she passed me the blunt that she had just fired up.

"I'm gonna get the fuck away from them." I responded.

I wasn't sure how the situation would play itself out, but I found out as soon as I turned off the street and the red, white, and blue lights lit up the back of the car. I was in no mood to be trying to outrun the police at that moment, but since I didn't have a choice in the matter, I put my foot on the gas.

"Day! Day! It's like three cars behind us already; where the fuck did they come from?" She questioned.

I didn't have the slightest idea where the cars came from, so instead of responding I took the first right and put distance between the car that was right behind me. Knowing the city streets as well as I did, I made two more quick turns before crossing Goodfellow at Emma and entering St. Louis County from the city.

"Day they still behind us! She screamed.

"Please shut the fuck up and let me drive." I responded as I turned the music up to drown out the sound of her voice.

One turn led to another that led to another that led to another as I tried my best to lose the cars that were behind me. I wasn't sure as to how many cars were involved in the chase, but I had already counted five as I ran the stop sign at Lena and Jennings Station Rd. making a sharp right.

"Oh shit." I thought to myself as I looked down and seen that Miser was calling me. "Hey now."

"Where you at my dude?" He questioned.

"I got them people behind me and they on one. Where you at?" I responded.

"I'm by the chicken joint waiting on you." He replied.

"Good, cause I'm coming in hot and I'm gonna need you!" I shot back.

"Talk to me. What's the play?" He questioned.

"I'm gonna slide past you, so follow me and make a left at Ada Worley, then a left on Berkay, a quick right on Dotley and pick this bag up." I explained.

"I see you coming bro. I got you." He answered.

"Call me back when you get it." I instructed before ending the call.

After doing exactly what I told him what I was going to do, I tossed my goodie bag out of the window before making a left on Trudy then a right on Shannon. As I made another right on Cozens I noticed another three St. Louis County police cars joining the chase.

"I wish the bitch stop screaming." I thought to myself as I ran the light and made a right on Halls Ferry. Not concerned with traffic or the police, I made a hard left turn on Bluegrass and put my foot down harder on the gas pedal. The street ended at the gas station. After jumping the curb and racing across the lot, I e-braked and slid into Lewis and Clark making a sharp left turn.

Putting my foot back on the gas pedal with a little more authority, I watched as the speedometer started to red-line. My count was up to ten cars at that moment, but I paid it no mind. It wasn't the first time that I had that many cars chasing me, so I continued to pat the gas pedal to get every mph that I could get.

After checking my mirrors and passing my passenger the end of the blunt, I looked down and noticed my phone was lighting up in my lap. "Hey now."

"I got the bag bro. Where you at?" He asked.

"367 gonna make this right at Chambers, cause they got it blocked off." I answered.

"Watch out for the spike strips my dude, you playing with St. Louis County pimp." He warned me."Good looking pimp." I responded then ended the call.

"I'm going to jail." I thought to myself, as I exited at Chambers and noticed that I could only go in one direction. That told me that I was not really in control of my route anymore and that I needed to come up with another plan. I wasn't sure what I would do, so I let my mind run as I watched the road for spikes and continued to pat the gas pedal.

Knowing that Chambers ended sooner than later, I informed my passenger of what she would need to do when we ran out of road. I also knew that law enforcement's main priority was to catch the driver, so after I gave her all the information that I could to help her get away, we were almost at our destination. She looked extremely scared as I made the turn into the cul-de-sac.

"Let's make it bitch. Be safe." I explained as I exited the car from my side and jumped over the fence that look me in the opposite direction than I told her to go. I had never been in the wooded area that I found myself in, but I was unconcerned. My only thought was to get as far away from the police as I could, and as I ran for my life, that was the only thought on my mind.

I had thought that I had heard a helicopter over my head, but as I hopped over another fence I was certain of it. That put me at a real disadvantage, but I pushed it from my mind. To catch me, they would need everything that they had at their disposal, and as I continued to make my way through the woods it dawned on me that they were.

Layla must have known that I was in trouble because as soon as I stopped to catch my breath, she called to check on me. I couldn't understand anything she was saying after I let her know my situation, but I played along for a second until I heard something that sounded like the police getting closer to me. At the point I ended our call and continued my run.

"I'm fucked." I thought to myself as I hid behind a tree and checked out my surroundings. I could hear the helicopter right above my head, and that did not sit well with me. So much so that I fired up the piece of blunt I had grabbed out of the ashtray as I exited the car. I figured that if I was going to jail I would be good and high when I got there.

Leaving my hiding spot and running a little further into the woods I noticed that I was coming out of them on the other side and that the police were coming in from that direction also. That told me that I was almost out of options but it really didn't matter to me. Giving up was not something that I planned to do regardless of my situation, so I turned back in the direction I had just come from and continued my escape.

A few minutes later it seemed like the sun had come out in the middle of the night, as the spotlight from the helicopter beamed down on me and the pilot screamed for me to give up over the loudspeaker. I couldn't see anyone in front of me or behind me when I looked, but before I could take another step I felt the pain of someone putting their knee right into the middle of my back.

It hurt for a split second, but the pain from hitting the ground and having all of the weight of the person behind it falling on me took it away and brought about another series of pains that I couldn't begin to describe. I know somebody was talking to me, but both of my ears were ringing and my head was being pushed into the dirt with a force that was completely uncalled for.

It took a few minutes for all of my senses to start back working at full capacity, but when they did, I could see at least thirty police officers from both the city and county with their guns drawn all trying to talk to me at once.

"I should kill yo black ass and leave you out here." The officer holding my left arm informed me.

"That's what's up." I responded.

"Why you run?" Another officer questioned.

"Who was with you?" Another one asked.

"Where the guns at?" Another questioned.

The thought crossed my mind to say something smart back to her questions, but I decided against it. I wasn't sure if I would make it out of the woods in one piece if I started playing with them people, so I just kept my mouth closed until they got me back to the street where all of their cars were.

I had been arrested several times in my life, so after I got researched for contraband, I was asked several questions to figure out who I was. I almost didn't say anything in response, but one of the other officers was certain that he seen somebody else exit my vehicle, so I told them my name and social to get them focused on me.

"So why you run?" The officer holding me against the car questioned.

"I should break yo God-damned jaw you motherfucker!" Another officer threatened as he punched me in the stomach.

"Don't break his jaw." Another officer cut in. "Break his ribs." He explained as he hit me in the side with his baton.

I figured that I would get beat, because it came with the territory of running from the police. I had seen it done on several occasions and knew that when I got caught that I would be treated with the exact same mercy. It didn't bother me at all, but it took me by complete surprise when the officer that ran my name through the system came back and stopped my abuse.

"I know why he ran fellows. Put him in the car." He instructed before telling them that I had been on the run for more than a year and the charges that I already had to look forward to.

Several things crossed my mind as I got situated in the back seat of the police car, but I pushed them from my mind because I couldn't do anything about anything where I was at. All I had to look forward to was another vacation for my actions, but that didn't bother me at all. It never had and as far as I was concerned it never would. The life that I lived came with consequences and I was well aware of them before I started playing.

"I wonder how long they gonna hold me for this time?" I thought to myself before closing my eyes to take a nap.

Made in the USA
Middletown, DE
21 August 2023